Readers Love Kim Fielding's
The Tin Box

"The book is well written, the plot moves along at a quick pace, the situations are believable, and there were moments of cringe-worthiness, heart pounding lust, tears, frustration, fear, repulsion, and at last a HEA that was warm and fuzzy but so well deserved."

—MM Good Book Reviews

"When I finished the last page of this book, I had to take a deep breath and attempt to get my wayward emotions under control. This is a powerful story, it had me crying, angry, frustrated and mad. It also had me laughing and smiling and happy."

—Hearts on Fire Reviews

"Read this book. You will be a bigger person for having seen this story unfold in front of your eyes."

—My Fiction Nook

"What a talent this author has in bringing us such a dark and sad topic and balancing it with light and sweet scenes. By talking about a subject that isn't really touched upon too often in this genre and making us realize just how far we have come and just how far we still have yet to go. I thank you Ms. Fielding for writing such an inspiring story that I know I will never forget."

—The Novel Approach

"Bill's story is haunting and heartbreaking, but Colby and William are fun and heartwarming. The emotional extremes meld together perfectly and work together to raise this touching story to another level. I highly, highly recommend it."

—Reviews by Jessewave

"A truly memorable love story which also reflects on a history that I hope never repeats itself."

—The Romance Reviews

By KIM FIELDING

NOVELS
Brute
Good Bones • Buried Bones
Pilgrimage
The Tin Box
Venetian Masks

NOVELLAS
Housekeeping
Night Shift
Speechless

Published by DREAMSPINNER PRESS
http://www.dreamspinnerpress.com

Pilgrimage

KIM FIELDING

Dreamspinner Press

Published by
Dreamspinner Press
5032 Capital Circle SW
Suite 2, PMB# 279
Tallahassee, FL 32305-7886
USA
http://www.dreamspinnerpress.com/

Pilgrimage
© 2014 Kim Fielding.

Cover Art
© 2014 Paul Richmond.
http://www.paulrichmondstudio.com
Cover content is for illustrative purposes only and any person depicted on the cover is a model.

ISBN: 978-1-62798-543-7
Digital ISBN: 978-1-62798-544-4

Printed in the United States of America
First Edition
February 2014

Chapter 1

"HEY, MIKEY-MIKEY. I'm waiting on those figures you promised."

Mike Carlson looked up from the spreadsheet on his monitor and tried not to scowl at his boss. "I'm working on it. Marketing didn't get me their numbers until a half hour ago, and—"

"Sure. I can see that you're slaving away." Dan Kennedy took a bite of apple and chewed noisily. He leaned against the wall of Mike's cubicle as if he planned to stand there all day.

"So if you'd just give me a little more time," Mike began.

Dan took another bite and spoke with his mouth full. "Yeah. Fine. But Monday we're gonna have to work on the quarter-end reports, so we're not leaving here tonight until I get that spreadsheet."

"I have plans."

"Yeah, so did I." Dan shrugged and tossed the core at Mike's wastebasket. He missed but didn't bother to retrieve it. "That's life in the big city, Mikey. I told you I needed it done this week."

"I know. And Marketing was supposed to get me their stuff ages ago. I've been on top of them for days."

Another shrug. "Yeah. Marketing sucks. And you know what? They're all gonna head home at five tonight, and we'll still be stuck here." He gave a cheery little smile before wandering away.

Mike pictured himself chained to his desk—shirtless and sweaty—while Dan stood over him, wielding a whip. Not that Mike was into that kind of scene, nor was the boss his type. Dan was slightly pudgy, and when he left work every day, he plopped a baseball cap on his head backward, possibly to hide his incipient bald spot from the larger world. Also, he was straight. Now, Paul in HR—*that* was more like it. The guy looked like he spent all his off-hours at the gym, and his hair had thick waves that begged fingers to run through them, and… and this wasn't getting Mike any closer to finishing his work. Besides, Paul was straight too. And kind of a jerk.

Dan came by Mike's cubicle three more times, each time derailing Mike's concentration and forcing him to recalculate a string of numbers. It was nearly eight o'clock by the time Mike attached the files to an e-mail and clicked Send. "Here they are!" he shouted across the office, his voice echoing among the empty cubicles. "I'm leaving now!"

"See you Monday!" Dan yelled back.

Mike felt slightly guilty as he shut down his computer—although he got to leave, Dan was going to be there a good while longer, going over the files he'd just received. Well, that happened when you were a manager. Mike had happily avoided such a fate.

He left the building and stepped out into the warm evening. The rosemary shrubs that landscaped the islands in the parking lot made the air smell like an Italian restaurant. Mike was allergic to rosemary; he sneezed. One of the large overhead lights was burned out, and the others cast strange shadows across the tarmac. It wasn't the first time he'd walked through the parking lot when it was dark and almost empty, but there was still something eerie about the place. A sudden rustle from one of the bushes caused him to jump slightly, then shake his head at himself. Probably just a cat or a rodent, maybe one of those huge black beetles that reminded him of tanks with legs. Still, he couldn't shake the feeling of being watched as he unlocked his Civic and climbed inside.

He stuck his key into the ignition but didn't turn it. Instead, he sat in the stuffy silence for a moment, thinking. Then he pulled his phone from his pocket and brought up Jeff's number.

"Hey, Mike! Where the hell are you?" There was a lot of noise in the background, and Jeff was shouting.

"Sorry. Got tied up at work."

"Again? Well, look. We're just finishing dinner, but we're all going to head back to our place for a card game, so why don't you meet us there?"

Mike was tempted. He'd met Jeff and Cleve the previous year during a ski trip to Tahoe. Mike had gone solo and ended up sharing a table with them at a busy bar. They chatted, and when they discovered they lived near one another, they'd traded contact info. Mike still got together with Jeff and Cleve pretty regularly, usually with a small group of other people. He always had fun with them, but tonight he was tired. "Will you take a rain check? I'm wiped."

"Sure. I know how it is. Maybe next weekend, okay?"

They said their good-byes and disconnected the call. Mike still had that itchy-shoulder-blades feeling of someone watching him. He looked around, but the only other signs of life in the parking lot were the moths spinning in the lamplight. He probably just needed a good night's sleep.

There wouldn't be much to eat at home, so he did a quick drive-through on the way. He wasn't a kid anymore—thirty was a couple years behind him—and he was going to have to run an extra mile or two in the morning to work off the bacon burger and fries. At least his stomach was satisfied.

The parking lot at his apartment complex was well lit and full of cars but still managed to feel a little creepy tonight. Instead of stubby little rosemary shrubs, it was ringed with full-size trees, any one of which could have camouflaged something bigger than a cat. Hell, Mike's assigned parking spot was close to the dumpster corral, and you could probably hide a small army platoon in there. Or at least a good-sized street gang. Jesus. He wasn't normally jumpy, but he couldn't seem to shake the feeling tonight. Walking the short length of sidewalk to his front door, he felt like he was onstage with an unseen audience riveted by his every move.

"Security cameras," he mumbled as he unlocked the door. That was probably it. They definitely had them at work and probably had them here too. The apartment complex had a pair of nighttime security guards who zoomed around in an electric golf cart, keeping an eye on people's cars and making sure nobody used the pool after hours. Maybe watching weary residents trudge home after work gave the guards their evening thrill.

Mike felt more secure once he was in his apartment with the door locked and chained. He went into the bedroom long enough to remove most of his clothes. He was a lot more comfortable after he'd stripped down to his briefs. Not for the first time, he vowed that someday he'd find a job that didn't require a tie. He'd love to show up for work in jeans, a T-shirt, and a pair of comfy sneakers. Flip-flops and shorts when the weather turned really hot.

He detoured into the kitchen long enough to fetch a can of beer from the fridge and pretend not to see last night's dinner dishes still in the sink. He also ignored the little pile of bills on the kitchen table. After a long day crunching numbers, the last thing he wanted to do was deal with his own finances. Instead he headed for the living room, where he plopped down on his slightly ratty but oh-so-comfy couch and reached for the clicker.

It took him three beers, ninety minutes, and four or five trips through the channels to decide there was nothing on. A couple of shows held his interest for a few minutes—some spy thing with George Clooney and a travel show set in Scandinavia—but they ultimately bored him. He paused again in the middle of *Magic Mike* to stare at Channing Tatum's pecs, then decided he might as well give up the whole thing and switch instead to honest-to-God porn.

He powered off the TV and settled back on the couch with his laptop open on the coffee table. He logged in to his favorite site, the one he used when he wasn't dating anyone regularly and when a quick hookup seemed like too much work. Over the past couple of years, his right hand had been his best friend a lot more often than he'd like to admit. Fucking random guys was less satisfying than when he was younger, and he hadn't yet found someone to settle down with.

But tonight he wasn't feeling angsty about it. The beer had mellowed him out, the couch pillows propped him comfortably, and he enjoyed the squeeze and rub of his hand down the front of his underwear. In a while he might take his briefs off, but for the moment this was good. The two guys onscreen were really hot. The hunky one with the shoulder tats was licking the blond's asscheeks as if they were a favorite dessert.

And then the doorbell rang.

Not in the porn video. If the doorbell had rung in the porn video, it would have turned out to be a cute pizza delivery guy or a muscular repairman, and then there would have been a spirited threesome, and *that* would have been great. But no, this was Mike's irritating buzzy doorbell.

"Hang on!" he shouted as he paused the video. He jogged to his bedroom, where he slipped into the khakis he'd previously discarded. As he was buttoning up, the bell buzzed again. "I'm *coming!*" And not in the fun way either.

He fumbled with the locks and swung open the door. The woman standing there blinked. "Can I help you?" he asked.

"You truly are—" She cleared her throat and straightened her shoulders. "We need to talk."

Mike looked at her quizzically. She was taller than his five foot six, and she tended toward plump, with a face that made it hard to guess her age. If pressed, he would have said fortyish. Her light-brown hair was done up in a complicated braided bun, and she was dressed like an escapee from a Renaissance faire.

"Um... do I know you?" he asked. Maybe she was a neighbor. Oh, shit! What if she was the person who drove the Prius with the "Coexist" and "Globalize Peace" stickers all over it, and what if she'd backed that thing into his car? He did not want to deal with insurance companies and body shops.

She shook her head. "Not yet. But we must talk. There's an angry god, you see, and—"

"I'm not religious." Her phrasing was odd, and she sure wasn't dressed in regulation Jehovah's-Witness-wear, but that didn't particularly matter. Mike was solidly, comfortably agnostic, and the last thing he wanted was for someone to attempt to convert him. "I'm not religious and I'm also a great big flaming homo, so please take your evangelizing somewhere else. I bet the guy in 3B would love to hear it." The guy who still occasionally stole Mike's Sunday newspaper.

Mike started to close the door, but the woman looked upset. "No!" she said. "I have to speak with *you.* Michael Albert Carlson."

He was a little weirded out that she knew his name—including his detested middle name—and he was therefore even more determined to get rid of her. "I don't know what you're talking about. Go away, please, before I call security." He shut the door very firmly and made sure to lock it.

He waited a few minutes, but the bell didn't ring again. When he glanced through the kitchen window, which looked out at the building's front, nobody was in sight. Good. Maybe this was some kind of new sales technique. He wouldn't put it past those satellite companies that were always trying to get him to switch from cable, and he'd noticed the carpet-cleaning outfits had been getting more aggressive lately too.

It took some time to settle down after that. Another beer might have helped, but he was out. Since his erotic mood was thoroughly broken, he flipped through the channels twice, finally watching the second half of one of those cooking competitions. The winner was a short guy who managed to make an edible dessert out of haggis, black licorice, and soy sauce.

Midnight was near, and Mike knew he should go to bed. He even went so far as to brush and floss. But he was twitchy and just sort of... off, so he ended up back on the couch in his underwear. He clicked on his laptop and watched the hunky guy and the blond go at it for a while. The blond was admirably flexible.

Mike's cock was hot and hard in his hand, slick with precome, and his balls throbbed with the beat of his pulse. He was good at this. He could jerk off quickly or make it last, according to his mood. Tonight he aimed for making it last, pausing his strokes whenever he got too close to the edge. Sweat dripped down his face and chest; it tickled his ass under the cloth of his briefs, which he'd never gotten around to removing. The guys on the laptop screen both shot their loads—messily—and the video ended, but Mike just closed his eyes and imagined a few of his favorite scenarios. A big man with a hairy chest bending over and waving his muscular ass invitingly. That same big man spooning behind Mike, broad chest against Mike's back, nibbling on Mike's ear and slowly, exquisitely working Mike's cock.

"Oh God, yes," Mike moaned. He was very close. Now if his imaginary man would only twist his wrist like *so* and do *this* with his thumb—

"We must talk, Michael Albert Carlson."

Mark screamed as he launched from the couch and landed in a shocked heap on the floor. His underwear was pulled down around his thighs, hobbling him, and his brain had pretty much cut all communication with his body. The Ren-faire lady stood very close by, looking down at him. Her face was sternly set, but amusement glittered in her eyes.

"How?" he finally managed. It was as close to coherent as he could get.

"You invited me in," she answered primly.

"I... I did not! I told you I was gonna call security!" With some difficulty, he got to his feet and pulled up his briefs. He was aware of his racing heart and shallow breathing.

"And then you called me. I heard you."

"I didn't— I don't even know your name!"

"Oh, the title will do nicely." She took a few steps closer to the coffee table and bent her head to look at the laptop, which Mike had knocked somewhat askew during his panic. He must have also pressed a button inadvertently, because a new video had begun. The hunky tattooed guy was now enthusiastically sixty-nining with a dark-skinned man. "Well, *that's* interesting," said Mike's unwanted guest.

Mike was struck with a revelation. "My sister put you up to this, didn't she? Well, ha-ha. You can tell her she really got me this time. And while you're at it, you can tell her I'm not speaking to her anymore, and next time Mom's on one of her *Why doesn't Marie get married and give me grandkids?* rants, I'm not stepping in to save her ass. Now, hand over the keys and get out of here." Why had he ever thought that giving Marie a set of his house keys was a good idea?

The lady's attention was still on the porn, but she flapped her hand. "This is about my sister, not yours."

"For God's sake, who's your sister?"

She glanced his way. "Yes, exactly."

Mike's ass hurt from landing on the floor, and his balls hurt from the orgasm-that-wasn't, and his head hurt, and he was tired. Maybe this lady was just plain old nuts... which didn't explain how she'd gotten into the apartment through a locked door. A locked and *chained* door. "What do you want?" he asked, knowing he sounded pitiful.

She turned away from the laptop to face him fully. She was smiling. "I want you to be a hero. A savior."

"By doing what? Going to your hippie church on Sundays? Making some kind of donation? Renouncing my heathen homosexual ways? What?"

"I'm afraid… it's going to be a little more difficult than that."

"More difficult than renouncing? 'Cause lady, in case my porn selection didn't clue you in, I'm riding the rainbow unicorn for sure. And I've been firmly in that saddle ever since my sister made me watch *Dead Poets Society* and I discovered Ethan Hawke." His voice sounded slightly hysterical, but then, he *felt* slightly hysterical.

"Unicorns? I didn't think you had them here."

It occurred to him, rather belatedly, that he could call the cops. He looked around for his phone, but it was on the coffee table right next to her. He'd have to use the landline. "Um, look. I gotta… I'll be right back."

He started to edge away, but she moved amazingly fast and grabbed his arm. She was very strong. "I think it is better we have this conversation somewhere else," she said. "Away from distractions."

"Great! Let me go get dressed and I'll meet you at, uh, IHOP. They're open late." And it was located far across town, where the cops could scoop her up with a minimum of fuss while Mike cowered happily in his apartment.

She shook her head. "We are going to travel in any case. We might as well do it now."

"Travel?" he said. Or started to say, because before the word had fully formed, the woman's ordinary brown eyes became very extraordinary, all crackling lightning bolts and swirling stars against flashes of orange and indigo. Mike's ears filled with a buzz like a million angry hornets as every hair on his body stood on end. He tried to pry himself out of her grip, but it was useless. And then he got an odd feeling in his belly, as if his stomach were zooming and swooping like a deflating balloon. He smelled hot metal and ozone and burning meat.

His vision went completely, utterly black.

And then the sun was out, and all he smelled was dust and, very faintly, horse manure. He was standing in his briefs on soft greenery beside a rutted dirt road. The sun was high overhead, filtered through a canopy of tree branches. Birds tweeted. And the Ren-faire lady was next to him, calmly smoothing her skirt.

"Wha-wha-what," Mike stuttered. "*What?*"

She smiled sweetly. "Welcome to my world, Michael Albert Carlson."

Chapter 2

HALLUCINOGENS. THAT had to be the explanation. Some psycho prankster had slipped something into his burger before handing it out the drive-through window and wishing him a good evening. Mike had never been much into drugs—a joint now and then, occasionally some poppers, and of course a little alcohol, but that was it. He didn't know what was causing his current symptoms. Acid? Mushrooms? Jesus, what if it was something really toxic and he was lying on his apartment floor right now with drool puddling under his cheek and his liver turning to goo?

"I'm sorry," the Ren-faire lady was saying. "The transition is difficult on human bodies."

"Transition?"

"Between worlds, of course."

"Of course." He wasn't sure of the best approach for dealing with a bad trip. Were you supposed to humor the hallucination until it went away?

"I am Agata." She said it the same way Madonna or Cher might introduce herself to someone who should have already recognized her but whom she was humoring nonetheless.

"Hi. Mike. But you already knew that."

"Of course I did. I went through a great deal of difficulty to fetch you." She started to say something else but stopped, her ear cocked toward the road. "I think it might be best to move away from the road before somebody spots you."

He docilely allowed her to take his hand and lead him deeper into the woods. Leaves crackled under his bare feet. The deep shade was chilly. He wished he'd hallucinated more clothes.

They came to a little stream that burbled happily over mossy rocks. Agata sat on a fallen tree that immediately reformed itself into a throne, albeit a rustic one with little twigs sticking out here and there. "Sit," she said regally, waving at the ground in front of her.

Mike sat. He wasn't very comfortable. There were sharp pebbles under his ass.

"This is my world," Agata began. "We are currently in the kingdom of Dalibor. It's a rather modest little kingdom, but pleasant. You will be journeying through it to the neighboring kingdom of Nenahde, which is considerably larger. Fortunately for our purposes, Dalibor and Nenahde are at peace. In fact, the young king of Nenahde recently married the king of Dalibor's oldest daughter. There were huge celebrations. Dalibor sponsored a tournament that was attended by all the lords and ladies, and all the greatest knights competed for days."

Mike didn't understand this hallucination. He'd never liked fantasy. All that crap with the wizards and elves and unpronounceable names full of random apostrophes and misplaced consonants. And as for royal weddings... well, okay, maybe he had watched William and Kate get hitched, but only because he was dating a Canadian at the time.

Agata's face grew very serious. "Unfortunately, that tournament was the source of our problem. One lordling who attended managed to offend the goddess Alina, and as a result, she cursed his entire village. He could make amends but refuses to do so. That is why I brought you here."

He blinked at her. "Me?"

"Yes. You will make amends in his place. It requires a pilgrimage and—"

"Why me? Am I the Chosen One, like Buffy or Harry Potter?" He felt his forehead to see if he'd hallucinated a lightning bolt scar, but his skin felt the same as always.

"Not exactly. You're—well, perhaps it would be best if I simply showed you. I suspect that would be more persuasive than a description." As soon as she stood, the throne turned back into a fallen tree. "Come along. We've a walk ahead of us, and I'd like to arrive before nightfall."

He padded after her, following the stream as it wound through the trees. He'd never realized that hallucinations could be so detailed, but he could make out the dozens of shades of green and the dots of bright-colored flowers and berries. He smelled earth and water and growing things, and when they walked through a patch of something with thorns, his legs looked and felt authentically scratched. He even had to wave away clouds of tiny insects that kept hovering around his face, finding their way up his nose and into his mouth. He noticed with resentment that the bugs never bothered Agata.

His feet became sore after a while, and although the walking warmed him up a little, he was still cold. He concentrated, trying to conjure sweats and Reeboks, but they didn't appear. And he was still tired, and his stomach began to rumble. If he survived this experience—if his liver didn't disintegrate and he didn't choke on his own vomit—he would make sure never, ever to touch recreational pharmaceuticals. He came to a halt.

Agata looked at him over her shoulder. "We must keep going."

"Can't we just skip this part? You zapped me to another world, so why can't you just teleport us to wherever we're going?"

She sighed. "Because I must be very circumspect. I'm really not supposed to be doing this at all, so I am using my powers only when absolutely necessary. Right now, they're not necessary. You can walk."

"Powers? What are you supposed to be, my fairy godmother?"

She looked at him as if he were crazy. "There are no such things as fairies."

Well, of *course* not. Fairies wouldn't make any sense. "Then what? A witch?"

Agata drew herself up to her full height and glared. Her eyes did that lightning thing. In a deep, loud voice, she announced, "I am a god!"

His memory briefly flashed to Sigourney Weaver and Rick Moranis standing atop a skyscraper, her '80s perm whipping in the wind. "Gozer?" Mike whispered.

"I told you—my name is Agata. Hurry up."

Not Gozer. That was a relief, but still he found himself peering through the trees anxiously, half expecting the Stay Puft Marshmallow Man to come lumbering his way. Apparently his subconscious was a much stranger place than he'd realized.

At long last, when he was footsore and limping badly, the trees began to thin. Up ahead he could make out a broad field covered in neat rows of seedlings. Just at the edge of the field, another creek met up with the one they'd been following, broadening it into a small river. Mike realized he was very thirsty, so he knelt on the bank and dipped a handful of water. It was sweet and refreshing even though it had a slight metallic tang.

Agata frowned at him when he was standing upright again. "You can't go into the village looking like *that*."

He glanced down at himself. Bare chest, a pair of blue briefs that were now somewhat worse for wear, dirty knees, scratched and scraped legs. "I tried to imagine myself a warmer outfit, but it didn't work."

"Why in heavens would it?"

"It's my hallucination."

She shook her head. "I assure you, Michael, this is no dream." She looked thoughtfully across the field and then back at him. "I can't conjure you anything either, not now. Go back to the trees and wait for me. I'll be back soon."

He considered arguing with her, but she hurried away. Besides, resting for a while sounded like a good idea. He positioned himself at the edge of the trees so he could catch some of the late-afternoon sunshine. At first he sat on a large rock, but it was uncomfortable, so he soon moved to the ground instead. He drew his legs against his chest and wrapped his arms around them. It felt very good to be off his feet. He watched a large bug with green and pink spots trundle by as he listened to birdcalls. He couldn't remember the last time he'd simply sat without an electronic gizmo close at hand.

He'd almost dozed off when Agata returned—but you couldn't sleep in a hallucination, could you? She was holding a pile of fabric. "Put these on."

He took the fabric from her. The colors were all browns and heathered grays, and the material had that slightly uneven handmade look. "Clothes?"

"Of course!"

"Where did you get them?" Surely he had hallucinated something more interesting than Walmart, at least.

Agata looked slightly embarrassed. He had the sense that wasn't an expression she wore often. "I stole them from a farmhouse," she said.

"A god who steals?"

"Out of necessity, yes." She shrugged. "I'll grant them a blessing in return. Maybe next time the farmwife is pregnant, I'll give her twins."

"You can do that?"

"Of course. I'm a fertility goddess. That's why I had the power to bring you here now: it's spring."

It was summer, actually. Late July—in the real world. This place did look decidedly more March or Aprilish, however.

Mike unfolded the clothing and looked at it uncertainly before putting it on. There was a pair of trousers that fastened with wooden buttons, a long collarless tunic with billowy sleeves and a wide V-neck, and an equally long vest thing. The vest was decorated with embroidered floral patterns along the hem and front edges. It fastened with three wooden toggle buttons, and it also sported a hood. Everything was patched and frayed, and most of the embroidery had faded from red to pale pink. The pants and sleeves were a little too long for him, but at least he was warmer. "No shoes?"

"If the farmer owns any shoes, they are most certainly on his feet right now. And probably wouldn't fit you anyway. But here, you'll need this as well." She unfastened from near her waist a swath of silky dark-green fabric, which she wrapped around Mike's neck and lower face. When she pulled up his hood, only his eyes were uncovered.

"Are we going to rob a bank?" he asked.

"The people in the village must not see what you look like."

No use asking her why—he'd just get an answer that didn't make any sense. He felt a lot like Alice after she'd fallen down the rabbit hole. He hoped he didn't end up shrinking or growing, and he was most certainly going to avoid hookah-smoking caterpillars.

Mike followed Agata around the edge of the field and through a hedgerow, across another field that had been freshly plowed but not yet planted, and over a low stone wall. That brought them to a dirt track—perhaps the one near which they'd first appeared—and they walked down the middle. They passed more fields. Every now and then, they walked by tiny stone houses. A few people hurried to pull weeds or plant seeds before it got too late, and others carried water or loads of firewood into the houses. Everyone watched Mike and Agata, but only briefly before getting back to work. Nobody waved or called out.

The village was on top of a small hill. It was surrounded by an ancient-looking stone wall, but the huge wooden gate was unguarded and propped wide open. Agata and Mike walked right through. Inside the walls, the streets were roughly cobbled, lined with two- and three-story buildings. The buildings tended to lean this way and that, windows and doors were oddly placed, and narrow alleys appeared out of nowhere, running crookedly away. Houses with laundry hanging from the upper floors were jammed next to shops selling meat, housewares, bread. Apparently Mike hadn't managed to hallucinate city planning.

Agata obviously knew the way, based on the confidence of her footsteps. Within only a few minutes, they'd reached a square that seemed to be at the center of town. Three sides were lined with the fanciest houses Mike had seen yet, while the fourth was dominated by a columned structure that he guessed might be a church or temple. In the middle of the square was a large well; old men and women sat on benches near the structure, chatting. Agata was making a beeline to a stone statue near the well. The statue was a man on a pedestal with his back toward their approach.

She walked around the statue, stopped, and gestured at it. "See?"

Oh yes, he saw. The statue was slightly larger than life-size and sculpted of white stone, but clothing—richly decorated clothing—had been painted on, and there was a painted face and hair as well. The man had a compact, lean body. His chin was square with a deep cleft that was kind of a pain to shave, his lower lip was full but the upper one thin, and if his mouth had been open, it would have been clear that his top canine teeth were considerably longer than his incisors. His nose had a slight bump in the middle. He had deep-set blue eyes and slightly arched eyebrows. And although his sandy-colored hair was long and bound with a thin cord, the cowlick that defied all attempts at taming was still obvious over his forehead.

Jesus. Was he really so self-centered as to hallucinate a statue of himself?

"*That* is Lord Meliach," Agata said very quietly. "The man who offended my sister."

"It's me," Mike hissed back.

"Yes. And now you see why I had to fetch you specifically."

"I don't remember pissing off any gods."

Actually, the god in front of him looked ticked off at his lack of understanding. But not curse-level anger—more sighing and eye rolling, like his sister, Marie, when he insisted she join him for lunch with their mother.

"It wasn't anything *you* did," said Agata. "It was Meliach."

"But I'm him. He's me."

"Yes. But you are not the same person."

"Um…." God, he was so tired, and he couldn't think straight anymore, and he was really sick of trying to make sense of this crap.

Agata's expression softened a bit. She took his hand in hers— hers was calloused, he noticed, and she had dirt under her fingernails— and towed him out of the square and down one of those serpentine alleys. When they rounded a corner, he nearly tripped over a table that was placed in front of what looked like a café. Two other tables were set out as well, as was a small assortment of chairs. "Sit," Agata commanded, then pushed him into a chair. She disappeared inside. When she reappeared a few minutes later, she carried two large clay goblets. She plopped them down on the table before sitting across from him. "He'll bring us something to eat shortly." She picked up her cup and sniffed at it, then took a small sip. "Oh, that's awful!" she exclaimed with a grimace.

He pushed his scarf slightly aside to take a taste too, and had to agree. It was probably supposed to be wine, but it was more like vinegar. Still, he was very thirsty and intended to drink it. But Agata grabbed the goblet, set it next to hers, and stared intently at both. For just a second, her eyes sparked. She took another mouthful of her wine, but this time she grinned. "Much better! I shouldn't use my powers like this, but who can abide bad wine?"

"Could I have coffee instead?" Drinking hallucinated coffee was unlikely to sober someone up, but he could give it a try.

She shook her head. "There's wine or ale. And the ale tastes like piss."

He drank his wine. He was no connoisseur, but it was very good. The best he'd ever had.

A teenage boy came outside with his not-especially-clean hands full. He dropped a hunk of bread on the table, set down a pair of wobbly bowls full of something vaguely stew-like, and, after a moment's consideration, pulled spoons from his pocket. "'Thing else?" he mumbled. "We got cheese too, but that costs extra."

Agata answered. "This is sufficient." The boy went back inside.

The food was not very good: gristly meat, mushy vegetables, bland broth, and stale bread. Mike waited for Agata to zap some improvement into the meal, but she just ate, and then so did he. He was ravenous.

Over empty bowls and a second round of wine, Agata finally decided to explain in more detail. "You see these spoons?" she asked, setting them side by side on the table. "They were made from the same mold. A poor one, but that's immaterial. The design is the same, this little flaw here on the handles. They were once nearly identical, yes?"

"Um, sure."

"But now yours has a little bend to it that mine hasn't, and mine has this nick here. They are the same spoon, shaped by different events."

He nodded. He wasn't sure where she was going with this, but he understood so far.

She gave him the exact same smile Mrs. Warner gave him in third grade when he'd finally learned to write his name in legible cursive. "You are a spoon, Mike, and Lord Meliach is another. You were created from identical... well, let's call them molds. But then you were put in different places. Different worlds."

He wanted to remove his hood so he could scratch his head but didn't quite dare. He chewed his lip instead. "So you're saying… this Meliach guy is me, but in an alternate universe?"

"That's not quite accurate, but close enough. A human can't fully comprehend this."

"Are there infinite other mes in infinite other universes?"

She looked annoyed again. "That doesn't matter. All that's important is this world. And your own, of course, if you return."

If? He didn't like the sound of that.

But Agata was still speaking. "Lord Meliach offended my sister and refuses to do anything about it. I can't influence him directly. You know, free will and all of that. But the villagers are suffering, and I can't have that, can I?"

"I guess not." For someone who was so concerned about the villagers' well-being, she'd paid them surprisingly little attention. But he didn't comment on that.

"There are rules, Mike, rules that even gods must obey lest we have chaos. One rule states that a person must repent and ask forgiveness for his own transgressions. Nobody else can do that for him. But"—she tipped her head slightly and curled her mouth into a small smile—"rules have loopholes. You are such a loophole."

"Oh. Oh! I can do the repenting thing because I am Meliach, more or less."

"Exactly! You petition Alina to remove the curse and—if you follow proper form—she must grant your petition."

Mike took a big swig of wine, draining the cup. He set the goblet firmly back on the table. "Great. So what do I have to do? Say some prayers in that temple in the square? A few Hail Alinas?" He wasn't Catholic and had only vague notions of what the whole penance gig involved.

"I'm afraid not," Agata replied. She finished her own wine, then neatly stacked the spoons. She patted her hair as if checking the integrity of her braids. And then she smiled serenely. "To gain my sister's forgiveness, Mike, you must go on a pilgrimage."

Chapter 3

FOR A brief moment when Mike awoke, he hoped the dream was over and he was back in his own bed. But even before he opened his eyes, he felt the hard ground beneath him and the scratchy clothes against his skin, and he smelled hay and manure. He pried his eyelids open. The sun was shining through the holes in the roof of an old barn, illuminating the dust motes. He sneezed and sat up with a groan.

His exhaustion and confusion had hit him like a blow shortly after he finished his meal the previous night. Agata had droned on for a while—something about pilgrims—but he hadn't been able to make sense of her words. She must have realized the futility of the conversation and had led him through the town walls to a farm, where she showed him a decrepit structure that had probably once housed a few farm animals. "You can sleep in there," she said. "Your journey will begin tomorrow."

He'd been far too tired to argue, so tired that he'd fallen asleep almost as soon as he lay down in a dark corner. He hadn't noticed the bumpy earthen floor at all.

But now he was noticing it—his back was sore and his mouth tasted like dirt. He stood up slowly, trying to stretch out a few of the kinks. He vaguely remembered Agata warning him to stay inside the barn, but his bladder was urgently full, so he ended up creeping just outside and pissing against the edge of the little stone building. And as he was tucking himself back inside the trousers with the weird wooden buttons, he found himself facing a cold, hard fact: he was not in the middle of a drug-induced hallucination. He didn't know much about psychedelics, but he was certain that no trip would last this long, nor would it have such underlying coherence tying together the bizarre bits.

He returned to the barn and sat on an overturned barrow with a missing wheel and broken handle. Okay. If nobody had slipped LSD into his burger, two options remained, and neither of them was attractive. Maybe he'd blown a gasket and was now so droolingly insane that he'd completely lost track of reality. That left his body back in his apartment, now with his liver intact. If he was lucky, someone would check on him soon, and he'd be bundled off to an institution where the doctors would fill his veins with medicines having lots of x's and z's in their names and where he might eventually regain himself.

That scenario just didn't ring true. He'd always been remarkably mentally stable. When he'd realized he was gay, he hadn't felt especially angsty about it. He'd told his parents, and they'd responded with love and support (and, on his mother's part, a hope that he'd settle down with a nice boy and adopt children someday). When his father died of cancer, Mike had grieved, but he'd also found comfort in remembering the good times he and Dad had shared. When the love of his life cheated on him and then dumped him, Mike was philosophical: other fish in the sea. College stresses, tough times at work, tight finances—he'd gone through perfectly ordinary hard times and had weathered them all. Everyone called him levelheaded. Friends came to him all the time for advice.

But if he hadn't had a sudden psychotic break, that meant he'd fallen down the rabbit hole for real. Christ, he didn't believe in rabbit holes or alternate universes or pissed-off goddesses. A trip to another world wasn't any less terrifying than the prospect of psychosis, really. At least mental illness could be treated.

"I hope you slept well."

Mike jumped slightly—he hadn't noticed Agata entering the barn. She held a piece of bread in one hand and a chunk of something that looked like cheese in the other. "Eat these," she said. "It's the last meal I'll provide for you."

They were dry, but he ate them dutifully. When he was finished, she made sure his face was covered by the scarf, then led him back to the dirt road. She stopped not too far away, in a spot where the river passed very close. He knelt gratefully on the bank, drinking his fill of the cool water and washing his face, hands, and feet as well as he could.

He stood and squinted at her. "Why me, Agata? Why not one of the other Mikes?"

"I don't know. I needed one of you, and it was you I found. Fate."

"I don't believe in fate."

She smiled. "That doesn't matter. Fate believes in you." She reached up to readjust his face covering, and her expression became serious. "Keep this on until you reach Nenahde. You won't be recognized once you cross the border."

"What happens if someone does recognize me?"

"Word will get back to Lord Meliach. He will not be pleased to learn he has a twin traveling the countryside. He's a stubborn, selfish man, Mike. You don't want to cross him."

It sounded as if Mike's doppelgänger was an asshole, which worried Mike. If they were made from the same mold, did that mean Mike was an asshole too? He didn't think so. He had friends. He wasn't a saint by any means, but he didn't treat people badly. "Okay. I'll keep the scarf on," he said.

"Good. And you may have this as well." She reached into the folds of her skirts and produced a thin book with a red leather cover, which she handed to him.

He looked at it curiously. There were no words on the cover at all, and when he opened it, he realized it had been handwritten in dark-brown ink. The script was ornate and hard to read. *"The Traille to the Shrine of the Ladye,"* he said doubtfully.

"Yes. It's an account of the pilgrimage you are undertaking. It's over three hundred years old, but I daresay things haven't changed much. The road is the same." She nodded. "You will use it as a guide. It tells you where you must stop along the way—there are several small shrines as you go—and what to do once you arrive."

Great. It was an alternative universe Lonely Planet guide. He wondered if it mentioned gay nightclubs along the way. Unlikely. "How am I able to read this? Why are we speaking the same language? Things look pretty different here from back home, and I can't imagine you've had the same unlikely combination of Anglo-Saxons and Romans and French and everyone to create the same English."

"We call our language Yezzik. It's not a coincidence that it's identical to yours. What would I do with an alternate to Lord Meliach with whom I couldn't communicate?"

The headache was coming back. He decided to let his worries go. No use trying to make sense of things if he was psychotic, and if this was *real*, well, he had bigger problems than linguistic puzzles.

His stolen vest had deep inside pockets. He slipped the book into one of them. "Okay, fine. What if I refuse to go? I didn't create the problem."

"No, you didn't. If you refuse to go, the people here will continue to suffer. And I will not return you to your home."

"You're going to force me? That's not fair!"

"Nor is it fair that the entire village suffers for one man's arrogance. It's a lesson every god knows and every mortal should learn: life is not fair." She looked slightly smug.

He looked down at his bare feet. They were already filthy, even though he'd just washed them. Then he looked back up at Agata. "If I do this, will you promise to send me home?"

"Mortals make promises to gods, not the other way around." She tipped her head slightly. "But it is likely."

That wasn't altogether encouraging. But maybe if he did this pilgrimage thing and Agata refused to zap him back where he belonged, her sister Alina would. For all he knew, this place was lousy with deities and some of them were willing to strike a deal. For the moment at least, going along with Agata's plan seemed the best option. Not a good option, just the best of them.

Either her goddess powers told her that Mike had reached a decision or his eyes gave him away, because she smiled broadly. "Leave now," she said. "You don't want to waste daylight."

"Fine. Where are my supplies?"

Her eyebrows rose. "Supplies?"

"Yeah. Shoes, extra clothes, money, um… passport? Whatever I need for the trip." He didn't travel all that much usually, and when he did, he always used packing guides.

But Agata was shaking her head. "There are no supplies. A pilgrim takes nothing—that's an important aspect of the journey. He entrusts himself to fate, to the kindness of others."

Mike Carlson was not Blanche DuBois. And as he recalled, things hadn't worked out very well for her. "Nothing?" he asked a little plaintively.

Agata stared at him silently for a few moments. She looked directly into his eyes. He didn't know what she saw there; in hers he saw hints of sparks, like the aftereffects of gazing at a bright flashing light. Finally, she reached into her skirts again and this time pulled out a small cloth bag. She tossed it to him, and he caught it. It jangled a little. "Just a few coppers," she said. "They'll buy you a night or two of lodging in Nenahde, nothing more."

"Thank you." He stuffed the purse in his pocket.

She pointed down the road in the opposite direction of the village. "Just follow this. If you hurry, you'll reach the border before nightfall. The book will direct you from there."

"No yellow brick road?"

She frowned. "No, just dirt. Cobbles in the larger towns."

Okay. Alternative world goddesses didn't get pop-culture references. "I don't suppose you'll be coming with?" he asked.

"I told you. I cannot get overly involved. I've done too much as it is. But my sister...." She scowled. "Do *not* tell anyone that I have brought you from another world. I forbid it."

"Why?"

"Magic like that frightens humans. It makes them wonder too much what else the universe holds for them. And in any case, I don't wish Alina to realize too soon what I have done."

"What's the curse? I mean, I know I haven't been here long, but I don't see plagues of frogs or anything."

Agata looked suddenly furious, which was scary. "She has refused them death."

"Huh?"

"You—Lord Meliach wanted to make a good showing at the wedding tournament, because he is a vain man. He said prayers to my sister Alina. He promised her a sacrifice if she would bless him. And she did bless him, and he won his competition quite handsomely. But by the time he returned home, he'd convinced himself he'd won through his own great skill alone, and he did not follow through with his promise. And so Alina laid a curse on all his people—none of them can die."

"That… that doesn't sound all that awful. Sounds like a *good* thing."

"Idiot!" she snapped. "My sister did not grant them eternal health or the miraculous ability to heal terrible injuries. Even if she wanted to, she couldn't give them those things, because those things are not within her domain. But she denies them death."

Mike remembered his father, lying still and shrunken in a hospice bed with wires and tubes and beeping monitors everywhere. He remembered how drawn his mother had looked, sitting at the bedside for days and days. And he remembered his father looking at him through filmy eyes that had once been bright and sharp, and Mike had known then that Dad had given up fighting the disease that was eating him from the inside. The morphine was no longer enough. Death had become a release instead of a threat.

"I understand," Mike said quietly.

"Then go, Michael Albert Carlson. Beg my sister's forgiveness."

He went.

MIKE WAS in pretty good shape despite the desk-jockey job. But jogging through his neighborhood in two-hundred-dollar running shoes or hitting the gym before work to lift weights was not the same as walking down a bumpy dirt road with bare feet. His feet started to hurt pretty quickly, and then so did his legs. The homespun clothing was uncomfortable, chafing against his skin. He was happy his briefs protected him, although even they were making him itchy from grime and dried sweat.

He wanted his Honda.

He wanted to go home.

"Where's the damned ruby slippers when you need them?" he muttered somewhere around midday. The bread and cheese breakfast, hardly filling to begin with, had long since been digested. Which was another issue—no rest stops or Porta-Potties along the route. Just trees. And farms. And a few people, most of whom stared at him distrustfully before looking away. He didn't blame them. With Agata's scarf wrapped around his face and his hood pulled up, he looked sinister, like a medieval Unabomber.

At least the roadway followed the river faithfully, which meant he had plenty to drink, and when he needed a rest, he could sit on the bank and dip his feet in the water.

With no company and not much to distract him, he was left with his thoughts. Try as he might, he couldn't make sense of what had happened to him. He couldn't come up with a better explanation than insanity or real-life magic. And that made him uncomfortable because either possibility required a major shift in his worldview. He wasn't good at that sort of thing. When he was a kid, some of his teachers told him he needed to exercise his imagination more freely, but he'd resisted. He was a color-inside-the-lines kind of guy.

When he was a junior in high school, his English teacher made them read *A Connecticut Yankee in King Arthur's Court*. Mike hadn't enjoyed it. The premise was entirely ridiculous. It had seemed to him at the time that if Twain wanted to point out stereotypes about the age of chivalry, which was what Mike's teacher claimed, he could have just written a nonfiction book describing the sixth century like it *really* was. But that would have required research, and novelists were probably too lazy for that. Easier just to make stuff up.

Now, though, Mike found himself a Connecticut Yankee for real—or a California one, anyway. But unlike Twain's hero, Mike was not an engineer. Sure, he could work frigging magic with an Excel spreadsheet, but that probably wasn't going to come in handy now.

He missed the Internet.

The shadows began to grow long, and he still hadn't eaten. He passed lots of growing things, but he wasn't sure what was edible. Besides, he didn't want to piss off a farmer. He would have paid a thousand bucks for a decent taco truck.

He didn't come across many other travelers. Twice men walked in the other direction with carts pulled by donkeys, and once somebody on horseback passed him by. One time he came across a small group of people—a family, by the look of it, with small kids—sitting by the roadside and eating. They didn't look friendly and didn't offer him anything, so he kept walking.

But when the sky began to dim, traffic picked up. People were hurrying now, most of them in the same direction he was going. He wondered uneasily if the road became dangerous at night. Bandits, maybe. Or predators of some kind. Wolves? Goddamn dragons, for all he knew. Or hell, he could just stumble over a rock in the darkness and break his neck.

He was considerably relieved when the road rose a little and he saw an actual city ahead of him. It was surrounded by a wall like Lord Meliach's village, but this city was much larger. And the road seemed to lead straight to an enormous open gate.

By the time he reached the gate, the crowds had become quite thick. People were clearly anxious to get inside, but a trio of men in uniforms was questioning each traveler and taking their sweet time about letting them in. Mike had been to Canada and Mexico a couple of times; it was strangely comforting to discover that border guards here were as officious as they were at home.

The locals weren't very good at lining up. They clustered close, jostling one another for a spot closer to the entrance. Mike soon realized that the guards weren't just officious—they were enjoying themselves at the expense of the people trying to enter. A group of people inside the gate were hanging around nearby, laughing, catcalling, and generally having fun with the free entertainment.

"What's your business here?" the guard with the thick mustache asked an older man. The older man had a dog, a medium-sized mutt with lopsided ears, and was using a rope as a leash.

"I live here. You know that. You see me every day."

The audience inside the wall snickered, but the guard made his face go stern. "Then what were you doing in Dalibor?"

"Visiting my daughter what lives there and helping keep an eye on her babies. You know that too."

"Do you have proof of what you say?"

One of the onlookers shouted, "Yeah! We want proof!" and the others laughed.

The old man scowled. "Tomorrow I'll bring ya a dirty nappy or three. That'll be your proof."

The crowd approved of this response—they clapped and hooted. The guard was less pleased, but he impatiently waved the man through.

Next he questioned a middle-aged woman and her daughter, both of them carrying large baskets, and a beefy man who was missing one eye. The guards' goal seemed to be embarrassing each person as much as possible without overstepping the bounds of their duties. Mike seriously considered slipping out of the crowd and going around the city instead, but by now it was fully dark. He wanted a meal, a bath, and a bed.

"What's your business here?" the mustached guard demanded of Mike.

"I'm... just passing through. Planning to spend the night before I move on."

The guard looked him up and down very slowly. "Let me see your face," he ordered.

Mike wasn't sure whether there was still danger of someone mistaking him for Lord Meliach, but he couldn't think of a way to refuse. He pulled the scarf down to his neck and shifted his feet as everyone stared. He hated being the center of attention.

But that wasn't enough to satisfy the guard. To Mike's consternation, the man placed a hand on his sword hilt. "Passing through why? Where are you going?"

"I'm... I'm a pilgrim." Absurdly, Mike pictured himself in a tall buckled hat.

"Pilgrim, eh?" The guard smiled, which wasn't especially comforting. He had terrible teeth. "Pilgrimage where? Gonna go ask Agata for a bigger cock?" The other guards, the bystanders inside, and even some of the people waiting to get into the city roared with laughter at this witticism.

Mike felt his face grow warm. "No," he said with as much dignity as he could muster. "It's plenty big enough already." That at least earned him a few muted chuckles.

"Then which god are you honoring, stranger? Or were you lying about what you're after?"

"I'm going to Alina's shrine."

The guard narrowed his eyes. "You honor the goddess of death?"

"I guess so."

"You *guess* so. Don't sound all that devoted to me. Does he, boys?" The guard looked over at his colleagues, who grinned and shook their heads. The crowd chimed in as well, hooting derisively. He took a couple steps closer, proving that his breath was as bad as Mike had feared. "I think you oughta show us how committed you are to your pilgrimage, boy."

"How?"

"Pay."

Mike thought of the little bag of coins tucked in his pocket. "I have hardly any money. I... pilgrims are supposed to travel light, right?"

"Well, then." The guard's smile grew. Flecks of food were caught in his mustache. "You'll have to find some other way to pay. Whatta you think?" He looked first at his colleagues and then at the rabble inside. A few of them called out filthy suggestions that made Mike's ears burn and his stomach clench. The guard seemed to consider his options before he finally nodded. "Sing."

"Wha-what?"

"Let's see if your voice is as pretty as your face, stranger. Sing us a song."

The onlookers cheered their approval.

Mike's heart was beating very quickly. He was glad he hadn't eaten since breakfast, because otherwise he'd probably puke. He had a terrible voice—he couldn't even stand to listen to himself sing in the shower or when he was alone in the car. No matter how drunk he became, he'd never let anyone talk him into karaoke. The only thing that terrified him more than public speaking was public singing. "I... I can't," he said hoarsely.

All three guards pressed in close, each with a hand on his sword. Mike didn't know whether they could kill him for refusing. He didn't want to find out. "Sing," said the guy who seemed to be in charge.

Mike couldn't even speak. A lump had grown in his throat, and it was amazing he was even breathing. Maybe he *wasn't* breathing, actually—he felt light-headed, dizzy. He'd never fainted before. He wasn't sure now was a good time to start.

There was a bit of a commotion inside the gate, and the guards turned to look. A couple of big men were dragging a cart closer, accompanied by cheers from their pals. "Make 'im stand on here!" one of them shouted. "So's we all can see him good."

Hands grabbed Mike's arms and pulled him forward through the gate, then hoisted him onto the cart. Everybody stood back expectantly except the guards. They remained very close. The mustached one drew his sword. "Sing," he repeated.

For a long, horrible minute, Mike couldn't think of a single song. Not one. And then… he thought of one. Even as he was opening his mouth he knew it was a terrible choice, possibly the *worst* choice, and he was going to blame every fucking baseball game he'd ever attended, but goddammit, it was the only song in his brain right then, and those swords looked awfully sharp.

"O-oh say can you see," he began. The guards removed their hands from their swords, but the crowd drew closer. There were more people now too, probably passersby trying to figure out what the hell was going on. "By the dawn's early light, what so proudly we hailed at the twilight's last gleaming." His voice cracked and warbled, hitting every note except the right ones. And he wasn't even at the hard part yet. Maybe he should have let them kill him. But they hadn't, and so he kept on singing. He had to fake it in a few parts where he wasn't sure of the words, but that was hardly the worst offense he was paying to the national anthem. Everyone gaped at him the same way drivers gape at a particularly spectacular car wreck.

By the time he hit the high notes—or, more accurately, failed to hit the high notes—his knees were shaking and his mind reeling with horror. He was sure his face had a redder glare than any rockets ever did. But he finished the damn song and then stood there on the cart, breathing hard, head hanging.

After a brief and somewhat shocked pause, his audience erupted in catcalls, wolf whistles, and clapping. Someone shouted out for another verse. But Mike hopped down off the cart and looked at the guards. "That's all," he whispered. His throat was raw.

The guy with the mustache looked at him thoughtfully. The guard must have decided he'd forced as much entertainment from Mike as he was going to get, because he gave an irritable shrug, stomped back to the gate, and began hassling a young couple.

Mike tried to avoid the crowd's attention as he slunk into the city.

Chapter 4

MIKE HAD never felt so lost. He didn't even know the name of this city. The streets were dark and mazelike, they reeked of garbage and manure and sewage, and he had no clue where he was going. He could still hear the mangled "Star-Spangled Banner" echoing in his head.

He finally stumbled into a small square where torches illuminated a number of rough tables and chairs. Men and women had gathered, eating, drinking, and talking. His stomach rumbled. He gathered his courage and approached a middle-aged couple who were laughing quietly over their goblets. "Excuse me," Mike said.

They looked up at him and the man frowned. "No beggars allowed here."

"Oh, I'm not. I'm traveling. I… I've never been here before. Could you recommend a place I can get something to eat? And a room. Cheap. Please?"

Their expressions softened. "Try the Bearded Hare," said the woman. "Not fancy but good enough, and they won't cheat you."

"Perfect. Thank you. Um… how do I get there?"

They gave him directions, which he followed carefully. He ended up only a few yards from the gate where he'd first entered the city. He was considerably relieved to see that the gate was bolted shut and there was no sign of the guards. The crowds were gone too, although a few people still wandered the streets. It was simple to find the Bearded Hare once he knew where to look. A fair amount of noise came from inside the two-story wooden structure, and above the door was a sign painted with the image of a goateed rabbit.

After ducking slightly to enter, he found himself in a large smoky room that smelled of beer and grilled meat. An enormous fire roared in a hearth at one end, and fat candles sparked here and there on the walls. There were long wooden tables with benches, a pair of kegs on a shelf, and an open doorway leading to a kitchen. Maybe two dozen people were inside, mostly men but a few women. A man and woman in their fifties and a younger man who must have been their son were moving around the room, bringing food and drinks and clearing away dirty dishes.

The woman walked up to him. "Help you?" she asked. She seemed neither hostile nor friendly, similar to a tired employee working the night shift at Denny's.

"I was hoping you had a room available for tonight."

She gave him a quick, shrewd look. "With dinner and breakfast?"

"Yes. Yes, please. And a bath." He added the last because he realized that indoor plumbing and an en suite bathroom were probably too much to hope for.

And he was right. "No baths. Can get ya a washbasin and a rag. Eight coppers."

"Um, hang on." He fished out the purse. As she watched carefully, he opened it and counted the coins. Twenty. Maybe he should save them for an emergency. But no—he was hungry and exhausted and he desperately needed to sleep away the memory of this day. He handed her eight coins.

Without another word, she led him to the end of one of the tables, very close to the fire and with no one else sitting nearby. Within moments after he'd taken his seat, she plunked down his dinner in front of him: a tankard of ale and a terra-cotta plate piled with mystery meat and mushy vegetables. She gave him a hunk of bread and a spoon. "We'll get your room ready when we're finished with this lot," she said, waving her hand to indicate the other customers.

"Okay. Thanks." He dug into his food. It wasn't very good. Too much salt, not much else in the way of spices, and everything overcooked. The ale was warm and sour. But the serving sizes were generous, at least, and that was good enough. He was too tired to care about more than filling his belly, and he ate quickly. When he finished, his hostess and her family were still busy serving other customers. Mike decided he might as well take advantage of the downtime and pulled the guidebook from his pocket. As he looked it over more carefully, he realized it was truly difficult to read. The handwritten font was unfamiliar, and the spelling was inconsistent. A lot of the words were old-fashioned too. It reminded him of another high school reading assignment, *The Canterbury Tales*. His teacher had made the class read some of the fourteenth-century version before relenting and giving them a modernized one. That book had been about pilgrims too, he recalled, but he didn't remember anything it said.

He puzzled over the book until his eyes grew blurry. But all he got out of it was a list of specific places he was supposed to visit—minor shrines and holy spots, apparently—and a heap of unrelated stories and advice. The first shrine was located on a hillside near a village called Kutina. He was supposed to gather some flowers there.

Yawning, he put the book away. He could read more once he got near Kutina, wherever the hell that was.

"Your room is ready," the woman said at last. A few customers lingered, but her husband and son seemed to have things under control. Mike followed her through a small door he hadn't noticed before and up some rickety stairs. A short hall led to another door. "You'll have it to yourself tonight. No other lodgers."

It hadn't occurred to him that he might have roommates.

She pulled the door open and waved him inside. It wasn't exactly the Marriott. The ceiling was low and sloping; he'd have to stoop in a good part of the room. Six lumpy-looking mattresses took up most of the floor space. One of them had sheets, a patched brown blanket, and a pillow piled on top. A pair of tiny windows looked down on a courtyard containing an outhouse, a well, and a chicken coop. A single small table was jammed into one corner of the room, and a large bowl and towels waited for him on top. In another corner was an ugly ceramic vessel with a handle. Mike had the unhappy suspicion that it was a chamber pot.

"Your coppers bought ya breakfast in the morning," his hostess announced. "No noise tonight."

"I'm just going to sleep."

She nodded once and walked away. He heard her shoes clomping down the stairs.

Mike shut the door. She'd left him a single candle in a holder on the table. By that feeble light he undressed completely and did his best to wash himself with the tepid water and a little chunk of soap. But then he had no choice but to put his dirty clothes back on. He promised himself that as soon as possible, he'd have a better wash in the river. His mouth tasted gross, his hair was a snarled mess, and he needed a shave. Maybe before he left town, he could find the local equivalent of Walgreens and pick up a toiletry or two.

He blew out the candle and lay down. The mattress wasn't much better than the floor of the barn, but he fell asleep immediately.

A ROOSTER woke him up. No, several roosters, and they were having a contest to see who could be most obnoxious. Mike squinted at the window. The sky had just begun to brighten, but he could hear activity going on downstairs already. Somebody was drawing water from the well, and someone else was clanging pots in the kitchen.

He was suddenly hit with a painfully intense craving for coffee. He liked his with a little sugar and a touch of cream. He could almost taste it, rich and bitter, sliding down his throat and waking up his body. He doubted he was going to find coffee at the Bearded Hare, but he climbed off the mattress anyway and readied himself for another day.

He was still groggy when he ventured downstairs. Early as it was, several customers were already gathered in the main room and the owners were bustling about. Mike was cold and chose a seat near the fire again. The owners' son thumped down a tankard of ale, which was kind of disgusting at this time of day, but Mike drank it anyway. He also received a full bowl of something lumpy and porridge-like, a rye roll, and a plate of half-burned sausages. Not knowing when he'd get his next meal, Mike polished off everything. There were no napkins, and he grimaced as he wiped his hands on his trousers.

It was time to hit the road. He waited for the hostess or one of her family members to approach his table. Maybe they could tell him how far away Kutina was and how to get there. Instead, one of the other customers rose from his seat, strolled across the room, and collapsed onto the bench across from Mike.

When Mike was in third grade, his mother had dragged him along to his sister's gymnastic lessons. While Marie tumbled and bent and leapt, Mike was supposed to do his homework as his mother read. But as he sat next to her, he'd sneak glances at her book covers: hunky, bare-chested men with long hair flowing in the wind, usually clutching half-dressed women in their bulging arms. Mike had been too young at the time to understand why these covers fascinated him so deeply. In retrospect, Ethan Hawke had not been the first hint that he was gay.

The man who now sat across from him looked exactly like a cover model from one of those books, assuming the cover model had been drinking heavily and hadn't bathed in a while. This guy had thick dark hair, biceps and pecs that bunched under a too-tight tunic, and a lush patch of chest hair at the open neck of his garment. His eyes were green—and red, due to the drink—his nose was straight, his chin firm. When he smiled at Mike, he had dimples. Mike couldn't help noticing that a scabbarded sword and a sheathed dagger were strapped around his hips.

"Hello," said the man.

"Um, hi."

"I'm Goran. You?"

"Mike."

Goran scratched his head. "Strange name."

"I guess. Look, nice to meet you, but I have to—" Mike stood and started to leave, but Goran grabbed his arm.

"We should talk," Goran said.

Those were possibly the three most toxic words in the world—in any world. His father had said them when he'd called to tell Mike of his diagnosis. Benny had said them right before admitting he'd been fucking someone else for weeks and didn't want to see Mike anymore. Agata had said them before dragging Mike into a crappy alternate dimension where he wouldn't have any shoes. He didn't want to hear whatever this Goran guy had to say.

But Goran had a very strong grip, and although he was still smiling broadly, he looked resolved. Mike sat back down. "What?"

Goran let go of Mike's arm and waved at the landlady. "More ale!" he called.

Mike didn't want more ale. He wanted to leave the Bearded Hare. But he waited as the landlady refilled their tankards. She demanded something called a leeka in payment. To Mike's surprise, Goran dug a coin out of his tunic and handed it to her. Then Goran took a very long swallow of his drink and belched loudly. "Gets the innards going, it does," he said with a grin.

"Look. I really have to hit the road, so if there's something you want to say—"

"Hire me."

"Excuse me?"

Another long swallow. "I said, hire me. You're on your way to Alina's shrine, yes?"

How the hell did Goran know that? Mike nodded carefully.

"So I can be your guide. I've been there before, lots of times. Know all the places where you're supposed to stop along the way and even a few shortcuts." Goran winked.

"I don't need a guide," Mike said, although that wasn't exactly true. He had no idea whether he'd find his own way with only the book and occasional help from locals.

"Of course you do. And even if you didn't, you need a guard. I am a very good guard." To demonstrate, Goran leapt to his feet, pulled out his sword, and waved it around gymnastically. He certainly looked impressive, even though he swayed a little whenever he tried to stand fully upright. The other customers and the inn's owners ignored him, as if they were used to watching this sort of thing. He did a pirouette, lopped off the head of an imaginary opponent, and collapsed back onto the bench. He set the sword on the table before downing the last of his ale.

"That was great," Mike said, not wanting to piss the man off. "But I don't need a guard. I mean, I don't have anything for anyone to steal."

"Pilgrims rarely do. But you still need me to protect *you*."

"I do not," said Mike, but he was wondering what he needed protecting from.

"Of course you do. A pretty boy like you, traveling all by himself—"

"I'm not pretty and I'm not a boy!"

Goran grinned. "A pretty *man*, then. And you're no fighter, anyone can see that just by looking at you."

Well, that was true enough. Mike's last fight had been in second grade, when he and a girl named Jennifer Tucker had a pushing, scratching melee on the playground over who was next on the swing. But Mike was still offended. Sure, he was on the short side and his physique was more lean than bulky. Unlike Goran, he wasn't built like Conan the Barbarian. But he wasn't a wimp, and he wasn't helpless either.

Mike pushed his still-full tankard of ale across the table. "Here, have mine. I gotta go." This time Goran was too busy reaching for the ale to grab Mike's arm, so Mike made it out of the inn and down the street, heading in what he hoped was the opposite direction from his arrival.

But he'd made it less than two blocks before Goran came loping up to his side and grasped his shoulder. "You think singing is the worst thing that can happen to you?" Goran asked.

Mike felt his cheeks flame. "You saw…."

"Of course I did. Heard you caterwauling too."

"You didn't do anything to save me then." Mike wrenched himself free and continued on his way, this time more quickly.

But of course Goran had longer legs—he was a good eight inches taller—and he had no problem catching up. This time he spoke as they moved. "I didn't save you because you hadn't hired me yet. Besides, it wasn't such a big thing. People laughed and that was all."

"It was fucking humiliating!" Mike growled.

"And if you think that's the most humiliating thing that can happen to you, you have some unpleasant surprises ahead. Which is why you need to hire me."

Mike stopped in his tracks and glared up at Goran, who also stopped. "I don't understand why you're being so insistent about this," Mike said. "You know I'm a pilgrim, and I'm not supposed to have any supplies. I have exactly twelve coppers to my name. I'm not real up on the exchange rate, but I'm guessing twelve coppers isn't much."

"No, it isn't. But you have other ways to pay." Goran waggled his eyebrows.

Mike's jaw dropped. "You think—you think I'm going to pay you with my ass like some kind of *whore*?" His voice had risen considerably—several passersby laughed at his outburst.

Goran, though, just shook his head. "It's a very nice ass, but no, I had something else in mind." He moved closer and bent to whisper in Mike's ear. "You have a book. I saw it last night."

"Um… so?" Mike blinked at him.

"Pay me with that. After your pilgrimage is complete and you don't need it anymore." Goran seemed to be completely serious. For once he wasn't smiling and his eyes gleamed.

Mike thought about the slim volume tucked in his vest pocket. It didn't look like much. Except it was old and handwritten, and… what if the printing press hadn't been invented here? "How many coppers is my book worth?"

"Coppers?" Goran chuckled. "I know a man who'd pay ten dinarka for that book."

Still with the exchange rate issue. Mike had a currency-exchange app on his iPhone. It would sure come in handy right now. "Is that a lot?"

"I could live off ten dinarka for almost a year."

"Oh."

Goran held his arms out wide. "So? Am I hired?"

Mike had no reason to trust this guy. He could be lying about the book's value. And even if he was telling the truth, maybe he planned to lure Mike somewhere and steal it—possibly slicing Mike's throat in the process. Kindness of strangers indeed.

No doubt sensing Mike's feelings, Goran sighed. "I'll tell you what. Give me three days. If you're not satisfied with my services then, I'll go, and you'll owe me nothing. But if you *are* satisfied—and you will be—you agree to take me on."

"A trial period?"

Goran shrugged. "If that's what you call it."

Mike leaned against the nearest building and closed his eyes, considering his options. He could refuse, but then the big lug was likely to continue to hound him. He could say yes for now and try to ditch Goran later, but given Mike's unfamiliarity with the route, he'd probably fail. He could give Goran a trial and hope his neck—and everything else he treasured—stayed intact. He opened his eyes. "Fine. Three days."

Goran gave his biggest grin yet and clapped his hands. "Excellent! I promise I'll satisfy you completely."

Mike wasn't sure whether the double entendre was intended, and was afraid to find out.

Chapter 5

"SO, YOU want to show me how useful you are?" Mike asked.

Goran nodded eagerly. He reminded Mike of a dog his family had acquired when he was a kid—Harry the Newfoundland. Harry was big and handsome and eager to please but not especially bright. At least Harry's love of liquids had been limited to water—Mike had already caught Goran looking longingly into the taverns they passed.

"What do you need?" Goran asked.

"Toiletries." When Goran looked at him quizzically, Mike sighed. "A hairbrush. Toothbrush. God, clean underwear would be nice."

At least Goran managed to follow through with that much—sort of. He took Mike to a crowded little shop with a stooped, witchy-looking proprietor. She provided a wooden comb and a small bundle of twigs that, apparently, you were supposed to chew to clean your teeth. "Sweet gum," explained the old lady, as if that were a selling point. She also found him a cake of ashy soap, which she wrapped in cloth. These things cost him a copper. She sold straight razors too, but Mike took one look at them and decided he'd rather grow a beard. Goran boasted that he shaved with his dagger. Quite possibly the truth, but horrifying.

Mike tried to buy underwear, but apparently it hadn't been invented. Everyone here went commando, it seemed, except during very cold weather, when they piled on layers of scratchy wool under their clothes. Mike wasn't about to try that, and besides, he couldn't afford medieval long johns. To his dismay, he couldn't afford proper shoes either. He ended up paying two more coppers for a pair of flimsy leather sandals and eyed Goran's enormous sturdy boots covetously.

Their shopping complete, Goran led Mike through the city. It was a busy place, with carts pulled by donkeys or people, squares packed with market stalls, workshops where men made rope or blew glass, and lots of other activities Mike didn't recognize. People seemed fairly cheerful even though everyone seemed to be working really hard, and the air reeked from a hundred unpleasant smells.

After perhaps twenty minutes, they reached another city gate. There were only two guards at this one, and they looked bored. They weren't questioning anyone who entered or left the city.

"Don't you have to get your things before we leave?" Mike asked.

Goran shrugged. "These *are* my things."

"But...."

"I have my blades. They're all that matters." Goran strode through the gate, Mike hurrying alongside.

There was nothing much of interest outside the city—more farms and small houses, a steady stream of people coming and going. Goran kept up a brisk pace but didn't talk. Mike found himself wondering about his new companion. Did he have family somewhere? How had he learned to swordfight? Did he often take on jobs like this one? For the first time since this ridiculous adventure began, Mike was thinking about someone else as a real person, a human being with a past and needs and emotions, and not just as a minor character in a bad movie.

But Goran asked questions first. This happened at midday, when they stopped to rest their legs and drink from the river. Goran had chosen a peaceful spot for this, a sunny little meadow dotted by yellow and pink flowers and with rabbits bouncing here and there.

"If I had a bow, I could get us a meal," Goran remarked. He pointed his finger at an especially chubby bunny nearby.

"You'd kill one of them?"

"If I had a bow. Maybe tonight I can try setting a snare."

"But... they're cute."

Goran gave him a very strange look. "They taste good. Don't they eat rabbit in Dalibor?"

"I don't know."

"You're not from Dalibor?" Now Goran looked startled, as if it hadn't occurred to him that people could be from somewhere else.

"No." Mike sighed. "I'm from California." That wasn't enough information to violate Agata's orders, he hoped. He hated trying to keep track of too many lies.

"Calif… I've never heard of it. It must be far away."

"It is."

"And how have you come so far without a guide? You don't look as if you've been traveling far."

"I… well, Agata brought me." Again, skating on the edge of permissibility but not, he hoped, quite over.

Goran had very expressive eyebrows, although they tended to be obscured by unruly locks of hair. "Agata? The goddess Agata?"

It was a very strange conversation, one Mike couldn't have imagined a couple of days earlier. He nodded.

His guide whistled and shook his head. "This isn't good. Why would Agata help you reach Alina's shrine?"

"She said she was concerned about these people who've been cursed. Why? Is it weird?"

"It's… troubling. The Sisters do not get along."

"Great." Mike rubbed his face. "Just what I need. Celestial sibling rivalry."

Goran picked up a stone and tossed it into the river, where it landed with a *plunk*. "Why are you paying homage to the death god, Mike? I've known plenty of men who prayed to her, but you don't seem the sort."

"I… it's a long story."

"We have three days," Goran answered, dimpling. He was disarmingly boyish when he did that, although Mike had noticed some time ago that his black hair was shot with a few strands of silver.

Mike tossed a rock too, but of course his didn't go nearly as far. "How far to Kutina?"

"Late tomorrow, if we walk until sunset today and begin early."

"Then let's get started." Mike stood and brushed dirt from his hands.

THEY SPOKE very little that afternoon. Mike was in a foul mood—he was hungry again, and his feet hurt. The sandals protected his soles but didn't give any support. The road rose slowly but steadily, and the farms became more scattered, with stands of woods or chunks of barren rock filling the space between them. At some point they lost the river, and Mike worried about that. How would they find water?

Goran, on the other hand, was obnoxiously cheery, swinging his arms and humming to himself. "Did you pray for the death of your enemy?" he asked out of the blue.

Mike almost stumbled in surprise. "I don't have any enemies. There's a few people who annoy me, I guess, but I don't want them dead."

"Then what did you ask of Alina?"

"Nothing. I never even heard of her until a couple days ago."

"Did you do something to make her angry? To curse people?"

"Not exactly." After thinking for a moment, Mike decided it wouldn't hurt to tell him part of the tale. "But somebody else did. And I guess he's a selfish bastard who won't apologize. Agata seems to think I can do it for him."

"It doesn't work that way." Goran frowned. "A penitent must make the pilgrimage on his own behalf."

"Yeah, well, Agata thinks she found a loophole."

Goran was quiet for a mile or so, probably thinking that through. The sun was getting low on the horizon, and Mike hoped his guide had a plan in mind for dinner and a bed. Beds, plural, that was. If time was moving at the same rate back home, it was Monday night now. That meant Mike had missed a day of work without calling in, and Dan was probably royally pissed off at him—the quarterly reports were due. Excuses about quarreling goddesses were probably not going to fly with him. Christ, Mike was going to be unemployed when he returned home—*if* he actually returned home. Shit.

"Why did you agree to do this for Agata?" Goran finally asked. "Did you pray to her for something? Oh! Are you hoping for a child?"

"Can men get pregnant in this place?" Mike asked, aghast.

Goran laughed. "Of course not! That's ridiculous."

"You have no idea what ridiculous means, buddy." Mike sighed. "So no, a kid is not in my foreseeable future."

"Doesn't your wife want a baby?"

"What makes you think I have a wife?"

"If you're trying to please Agata, you must be hoping for fertility. And if you're hoping for fertility, you must have a wife. Oh! I see."

Mike was a little dizzy from Goran's reasoning. "You see what?"

"You don't have a wife because your cock doesn't work." He nodded. "That's what you want from her—to make your cock hard again."

"My cock works just fine!" Mike yelled. Which was unfortunate, because just then they passed a man and woman and small child. The trio gaped, Goran snorted, and Mike blushed again. He waited until the family was out of earshot before repeating—in a quieter voice—"I have no problems in that department. And I don't have a wife, and I don't want one. I'm gay."

"You don't seem very happy."

Mike was tempted to kick Goran, which would have been a mistake given Mike's flimsy footwear and Goran's considerable size and weaponry advantages. But then he realized Goran wasn't teasing him. "Not *happy* gay. Homosexual gay." When Goran still looked puzzled, Mike elaborated. "I'm attracted to men."

"Me too," Goran replied cheerfully. "Women are too... squishy."

Squishy. Mike had never thought of women quite that way, but okay. "So I like men and my dick's up to par and I don't want any kids."

"Then why... why Agata?"

For a moment, Mike considered spilling his guts and telling Goran everything. But he didn't really know this man and still wasn't sure he could trust him. And spouting off about alternate worlds and Lord Meliach might not be so wise even if Agata hadn't forbidden it. He settled on a partial truth. "I'm really hoping that if I do this, Agata will do something for me in return. And it doesn't involve penises or children."

"But you won't tell me what," said Goran, suggesting that he was shrewder than Mike had guessed.

"I'm sorry. No."

Goran didn't press the matter, but he looked disappointed. He let his head hang and dragged his feet a bit, churning up clouds of dust that made Mike cough. The sun had disappeared over the top of the next hill and the light had begun to fade when he asked quietly, "Do you have a husband?"

"No," Mike answered shortly.

"Oh. I did. Once."

"You had—"

But before Mike could finish his question, Goran bounded ahead, hurrying toward a squat stone structure with a front yard full of seedlings and a wisp of smoke coming from the chimney. It was the first house they'd passed in some time. Goran pounded on the front door, which opened just as Mike arrived at his side.

"Yes?" asked the wary-looking woman who peered out at them. She had a toddler on one hip and a large wooden spoon in her hand.

"Good evening," said Goran, and he gave her a small but definite bow. "My master is on a pilgrimage. We'd beg of you a meal and ale and a place to rest for the night."

She had the sort of expression Mike had when little kids came to his door selling cookies or candy or magazines for various fundraisers—annoyed but not willing to be an asshole about it. Her kid had a runny nose and looked as if he'd been crying. His bottom lip was still a little wobbly. The woman was still standing there when a man appeared behind her. He was carrying a child too—a younger baby—and looked even less happy than his wife. But she turned her head slightly. "Pilgrims," she said.

After a pause, he nodded. "There's a lean-to behind the house with clean hay. You can sleep there. I'll bring you a meal."

"And ale?" asked Goran.

"And ale." The man pushed the door shut.

The lean-to wasn't very big, and most of it was taken up by hay and farming tools. At least the hay would be more comfortable than bare ground, Mike hoped. He settled down and took off his sandals so he could rub his feet. Goran plopped down next to him without bothering to remove his weapons. "See? I've helped you already," he said.

"I could have asked them by myself."

"But they might have refused. You look more important with a guard."

Mike doubted that he looked important ever but didn't say so. Besides, the man of the house came out just then. He silently handed Goran a basket and then quickly walked away. The basket proved to contain a couple bowls of watery stew, a small loaf of brown bread, and a chunk of slightly moldy cheese. There was also a metal bucket full of ale. There were no cups or cutlery.

While Mike slurped at his stew, Goran chugged ale. Some of it dripped down his chin, but he didn't seem to care. He drank an enormous amount, belched, and set the bucket down. "The Bearded Hare had better," he said as he tore off a piece of bread.

Mike was hungry and thirsty enough that he didn't care how anything tasted. He simply ate and drank. Goran did the same, taking most of the ale for himself and then looking mournfully into the empty container. "Wish there was more."

"If you drink more, you'll be drunk."

"I know."

After that, they said little. They each made a quick trip away from the house to empty themselves; then they lay down on the hay a few feet apart. Mike used Agata's scarf as a small makeshift blanket. Goran must have been comfortable enough without, because within moments he was snoring softly. Mike fell asleep soon after.

MIKE HATED goddamn roosters. He was sure of that fact despite his general disorientation as he sat up and peeled his eyes open—first trying to remember where the hell he was, and then wondering where Goran had gone. More bread and cheese had materialized in the basket while he slept, along with some kind of egg-and-milk-and-herb thing that was tasty enough to make him reconsider his antipathy toward chickens. There was a bucket about one-fifth full of ale, which Mike finished off. He attempted to tame his hair with the wooden comb and chewed one of his tooth-cleaning sticks. The stick did freshen his breath, but he didn't know whether it did anything for general dental hygiene. He hoped he didn't end up with serious problems, because if he was unemployed when he returned, it also meant the loss of his dental insurance.

He was still thinking about his teeth when Goran appeared around the corner of the house. He was grinning and carrying what appeared to be a hunk of raw meat. When he got closer, Mike saw that it was, in fact, a dead and skinned rabbit. "Dinner," Goran announced. "We can use your scarf to wrap it in."

"I thought you needed a bow."

"Borrowed a sling from our host. He uses it to scare birds from the fields. Are you ready to go?"

"Yeah, I guess." Mike's muscles were sore, and he wasn't all that happy about using the scarf to carry a bloody carcass. But real meat for dinner would be nice. So instead of arguing, he stretched and nodded. "Let's go."

The farm couple was standing in front of the house when Mike and Goran came around. But their demeanors had improved considerably—they were now smiling widely. They even waved as Mike and Goran left. "Why the change in attitude?" Mike asked when they were a little way down the road. He gestured back at the couple to show who he meant.

"Caught them some rabbits too. Eight of them. There are a lot of rabbits around here! That family will eat well for several days."

"Why'd you do that?"

"Don't like to be a burden," Goran replied. He wasn't looking at Mike.

Mike decided to file that away for later pondering. He still didn't know what to make of his companion.

An hour or so into that day's journey, the landscape began to change. The shady forests segued into small stands of scrub, and the cropland disappeared entirely. Instead, sheep and goats nibbled at pale greenery growing among the rocks. Mike and Goran didn't pass through any towns, just occasional clusters of a few stone houses. Each of these clusters had a well where the travelers paused for a drink. Goran frowned, looking as if he were wishing for something stronger than water. In the early afternoon, they passed some jagged rocks bigger than any mansion. The sun had grown warm by then, so they chose a spot where the rocks offered a bit of shade. Goran gathered twigs and used a flint to start a fire, then stuck the rabbit in the flames to cook. He sat next to Mike to wait for lunch.

"You'd make a great Boy Scout," Mike observed after a long stretch of silence.

"What's that?"

"It's… nothing. Something back home."

Goran shot him a sidelong glance. "You miss your home."

"God, yes." A thought occurred to Mike a moment later. "Where's your home? That city at the border?"

"No. I wander." Goran stared down at his big hands and sounded wistful.

"But where are you from?"

"Far. Maybe not so far as you, though." He got up to poke at the fire and rearrange the rabbit. The meat was starting to smell good, making Mike's mouth water. But it must not have been cooked enough, because Goran sat back down. "You don't have a husband, but you must have family who miss you."

"Yeah. Me and my mom and my sister—we argue, but we love each other."

"Do they know where you are?"

Mike's stomach clenched. He hadn't even thought about them. Probably by now they'd noticed he'd gone missing, and they must be frantic. It wasn't Mike's style to disappear without saying anything. Although his trip to this world had been entirely involuntary, he felt guilty about causing his family grief. His friends would be worried too. Crap. "No," he whispered.

Goran patted Mike's shoulder. "You'll complete your pilgrimage, and you'll see them again soon. Imagine the stories you'll be able to tell them about what you've seen!"

Stories that would get Mike committed. But he managed a small smile for Goran. "How about you?"

"No family." And that must have been an uncomfortable subject too, because Goran suddenly rose. He walked quickly around the rock and out of sight. Maybe he just had to take a piss, but he was gone a long time. When he returned, he checked their meal and pronounced it ready.

Half the rabbit was burned and the other half still fairly raw. They had no cutlery except for Goran's dagger, no plates or napkins. But the meat tasted good and filled Mike's stomach, so he couldn't complain. He hadn't eaten anything cooked over a campfire since his family spent a long weekend at Yosemite when he was a little kid. It was a good memory. They'd enjoyed hiking around the waterfalls and scrambling over rocks. Then, in the evenings, they cooked hot dogs and s'mores. They'd seen bears. Marie got a sunburn and Mike fell and skinned a knee, and at night their dad told them ghost stories and they slept in a tent.

Buoyed by a good meal and happy recollections, Mike started the afternoon portion of the walk in a better mood. Goran seemed to have shaken off whatever upset him earlier. He was humming again. Sometimes he pointed out things he thought might interest Mike, such as a large bird with red-and-black plumage and a prickly plant Goran said was useful for treating wounds.

As the day grew later, they approached a village. It didn't have a wall around it, and the streets were unpaved. The locals were dressed more raggedly than Mike. They eyed Goran apprehensively, clearly hoping he'd move on quickly. But he stopped in front of a tiny building instead. "Buy us dinner?" he asked Mike.

Mike hadn't even realized they were at an inn. There was no sign. "I told you. I have very little money."

"But you have enough for two meals."

"Yes. But I need to save it."

"Why?"

"In case I need it later," Mike said, slightly exasperated.

"You could die tomorrow. Enjoy what you have while you can."

That was a cheery thought, and it ran contrary to Mike's fiscal-analyst heart. But Goran looked stubborn, and Mike was suddenly afraid of being abandoned. His guardian had proven much more helpful than he'd anticipated. "Fine," he grumbled.

As it turned out, Goran ate very little, choosing to drink his dinner instead. After forcing down the slop that passed for stew in this dirty little place, Mike wondered if Goran hadn't chosen the wiser route. But no, Mike needed to be sober for the shrine, and according to Goran, Kutina was very near. Goran, however, was obviously pretty buzzed by the time they hit the road again. His steps were unsteady and his path tended to veer. He mumbled to himself too, snatches of words Mike couldn't understand. Once Goran tripped over a large rock and barely avoided landing flat on his face, and after they'd left the village and were heading up a steep hill, he pulled out his sword and swung it randomly through the air. Alarmed, Mike kept a safe distance away.

There were no signs of habitation here at all, not even any sheep. Just stones and scrub and dirt and the sky tinged orange and red with the setting sun. Mike worried that they were lost… or worse. If Goran actually intended to slit Mike's throat, this would be a fitting spot.

But as they crested the hill, Mike realized that the scattered boulders were in fact the ruins of what had once been a good-sized town. None of the structures were even remotely intact, but a few walls remained in a half-tumbled state and some foundations were visible beneath the weeds. They even passed a broken fountain with bits of intricate mosaic around its base. "Kutina?" Mike asked Goran, who was several paces ahead of him.

"Yes."

"What happened here?"

"War. A long time ago." Goran seemed very sober now.

It made sense that the goddess of death would have a shrine in a place like this—a dead city. Mike wondered what the war had been over. Did anyone remember? Did it matter anymore?

At the far end of the ruins, a single small building still stood— barely. It leaned crookedly, and the building stones were cracked and chipped. The figures carved into the walls were too worn to make out. "Doesn't look up to code," Mike said.

Goran frowned at him. "What?"

"Nothing. Okay. The book says I'm supposed to make an offering of flowers." Mike looked around and noticed wildflowers blooming here and there. "Any specific kind?"

"No."

Goran sat on what looked like the pedestal of a broken column, and he watched as Mike gathered flowers. Looking closely, Mike realized there were several species. He didn't know if any of them existed in his own world—he knew nothing about botany or gardening. Back when he and Benny were dating, they used to spend hours talking about buying a house someday, and Benny would drone on about what he wanted to plant there. Mike never paid much attention to the words, although he'd enjoyed watching the enthusiasm on his lover's face. Christ, Mike had almost forgotten about those conversations and the deep comfort he'd felt when entwined with Benny on the couch, dreaming about the future. A future that never happened.

"Is this enough, do you think?" Mike held up a healthy handful of blooms in pink, yellow, purple, and white.

"Probably."

Deciding it was the best answer he was likely to get, Mike cautiously entered the shrine. The floor was stone, littered with dirt and dried leaves that had drifted in. There were no adornments except for a statue up against one wall. Mike couldn't make out the details at first—it was quite dark inside—but when he got closer he saw that it was a woman who resembled a thin version of Agata. She was smiling, but it wasn't a pleasant smile. Shivering a little, Mike set the flowers atop the pile of dead stuff at her feet. It was a big pile of former offerings, long ago turned brown and black. He'd thought flowers an odd thing to bring to a death god, but now it made sense—the bright flowers of his offering were already wilting, the first stage of their demise.

The guidebook hadn't said anything about a prayer. "Gonna have to wing it," Mike muttered. And then he said more loudly, "Hello, um, Lady Alina." Was that how you addressed a goddess? Somehow his scattered childhood etiquette lessons had never covered that subject. "Please accept these flowers as my gift. And please accept my apologies for… for your being slighted after the wedding tournament. Um… amen."

He backed quickly out of the shrine.

Goran was standing and waiting for him, his body dark against the last of the day's light. Mike couldn't make out his expression. "I guess we're done here," Mike said. "Where are we going to sleep?"

"Not here. Too many ghosts."

Mike didn't believe in ghosts. Of course, he also didn't believe in alternate universes and feuding gods.

The pathway down the hill was treacherous in the dark. Mike stumbled a few times. One of those times he certainly would have fallen if Goran hadn't caught him in his strong, steady arms. Warm arms, Mike couldn't help but notice as he righted himself. "Thanks," he mumbled.

"It's my job."

At the base of the hill, Goran simply plopped himself down on a spot of relatively rock-free ground. He lay down at once, again not bothering to remove his weapons or boots. There was something oddly forlorn about the big man curled like that, with nothing around him but emptiness. Emptiness and Mike.

Sighing, Mike lay a few feet away. This was his most uncomfortable bed yet, but at least the night was balmy, and he didn't need the bit of extra warmth the scarf could provide. The scarf was still bloodstained from the rabbit; he'd crumpled it and shoved it in his pocket. It smelled, but then so did he. He really, really wished for a bath and clean clothing.

"Mike?"

Mike wondered why Goran was whispering when there was nobody but them for miles. "Yes?" Mike whispered back.

"I know it hasn't been three days yet, but—"

"You're hired. You've passed your trial period with flying colors."

"Thank you." Goran's voice was tight with emotion, but Mike couldn't tell *which* emotion. "Good night, Mike."

"Night, Goran."

Chapter 6

THERE WERE no roosters this morning, which was good. But there was also no breakfast, not even water to drink, and Mike's body had reached new levels of soreness after a night on the bare ground. He would have sold his soul for an air mattress. Goran, of course, was cheery again. He bounced impatiently, waiting for Mike to comb his hair and gnaw on his tooth stick. After Goran emptied his bladder, his entire morning grooming ritual consisted of running his fingers through his long hair and then retying the leather cord that attempted to bind it.

"Where do we go next?" Goran asked while Mike adjusted a sandal strap.

Mike looked up at him sharply. "I thought you knew. You're my guide. Been this way lots of times, you said."

Goran's grin was not at all chagrined. "I exaggerated. I have traveled nearly everywhere in Nenahde at one time or another. But I never exactly made the pilgrimage."

"Then why the hell—"

"You needed a guard. I needed a job. Doesn't matter if I don't know the exact route we're meant to take—your book tells you that. I can help keep you safe and find you food and places to sleep." He spread his arms. "You've seen that already."

Mike was tempted to be angry. But Goran was telling the truth; he had already proven himself helpful. And if Mike was honest with himself, he enjoyed having company. It had been a long while since he'd spent more than a couple hours with anyone except coworkers, and he was finding the companionship pleasant.

He tossed his tooth stick away and pulled the book from his vest. "Fine. But no more lies, okay?"

"Not even polite ones, like, *Yes, Mike, you are very agreeable first thing in the morning?*"

Mike tossed a pebble at him. He missed, which made Goran laugh.

After wiping his hands as clean as possible on his trousers, Mike opened the book. He skipped over the first few pages, which were about Kutina, then slogged through several paragraphs in which the author inexplicably decided to discuss his views on whether young people should choose their own spouses or allow their parents to choose for them (the author favored the latter). Mike briefly wondered whom his mother would pick for him. She'd never much cared for Benny, even before he broke Mike's heart, but at this point she'd probably pounce on the nearest available suitor.

"Okay," Mike said after a while. "I guess next we're supposed to go somewhere named, um, Ugolin. Does that sound familiar?"

"Yes. I know it."

"Is it far?"

"Four days. Perhaps five."

"Great." Mike sighed before peering at the text again. "I'm supposed to make some kind of offering there, but I can't make out this word. Can you?" He held the book toward Goran.

Goran hung his head. "I can't read."

"Oh." Such a possibility had never occurred to Mike. But now that he thought of it, he'd seen very little writing anywhere, not even on shop signs, which relied mostly on pictures. Maybe literacy wasn't very common in this place. "I'm sorry. I hadn't realized. Where I'm from, everyone learns to read."

"You do?"

"Yeah. We have schools. There are even laws that say you have to go until you're eighteen."

"*Everyone* goes? Even the poor? Even children with no families?"

"Everyone. Some schools are a lot better than others, of course. In my town, the schools in the poor part of town were definitely crappier than near me. Older, kinda run-down. Some didn't even have air-conditioning."

"Air-conditioning?"

"It's… never mind." Mike closed the book, tucked it away, and stood. "This book is not as helpful as it should be. I'd give it, like, two stars at best. I guess we can just head to Ugolin and figure things out from there."

Goran nodded. "Good." He took off at a quick pace that left Mike struggling to keep up.

THE LANDSCAPE didn't change much over the next few days, which left them few options for food and shelter. But Goran always found a place to beg a meal—and ale. The locals weren't exactly thrilled to be donating, but they always gave a little. And when he could, Goran performed some small service in return, such as gathering firewood or spending an hour hauling rocks out of someone's pathetic attempt at a vegetable garden. Judging from the expressions on people's faces, Mike guessed that Goran's services were quite unexpected. When he asked Goran why he did them, his guard only shrugged and repeated, "I like to be useful."

The people here were poor. Not college poor, as Mike had experienced when he was a student sharing a crappy apartment with four other men and living off ramen noodles, but truly poor. No shoes, not even thin-soled sandals like his. Rags for clothing. Tiny houses in disrepair, with skinny dogs and skinny goats and skinny chickens and skinny children. The kind of poverty that meant doing backbreaking work from dawn until dark and still not having enough food to feed the family. He knew there were places in his world where people had this little, but he'd never seen them firsthand. He felt ashamed for all the times he'd whined about his own minor misfortunes such as slow Wi-Fi or malfunctioning espresso machines.

"I wish I were a Connecticut Yankee," Mike said on the third afternoon, shortly after they'd passed through a tiny hamlet even more miserable than the last. Goran was drunk, because although there was no inn, a haggard-looking woman had given them a jug full of liquor. It had belonged to her husband, who'd recently died. Quite possibly the liquor had killed him, Mike thought, because the stuff was vile. Goran drank it anyway. Mike had looked at the woman and her three small children, and he'd given her all but his last two coppers.

"Wish you were what?" Goran asked. He was slurring his words a little.

"I wish I could… help. Where I come from, we have machines, medicine. Irrigation. Some of those things would really improve lives around here. But I don't know how to create them."

"Your country must be wonderful."

"In some ways, yeah. I suppose so."

"And you miss it." Goran slung an arm around Mike's shoulders and squeezed—not especially gently. "I'm sorry."

"It's okay."

Goran didn't remove his arm. It was heavy, and he smelled like sweat and dirt and alcohol. But Mike was pretty ripe himself, and he kind of liked walking like this. It had been ages since anyone had touched him more than briefly. He wrapped an arm around Goran's waist and told himself it was only to keep his intoxicated companion upright and moving forward.

It had been hours since they'd last passed any sign of human habitation, and Goran had long since sobered up. The road had been gradually rising for the past two days, and the setting sun illuminated an impressive-looking peak ahead of them. "We'll climb that tomorrow," said Goran. "Ugolin's not far away on the other side."

"Okay." Mike looked at the barren landscape around them. "I guess that means we're sleeping here tonight."

Goran shrugged. "At least it's warm. And dry. Have you ever spent days and days out in the rain and then tried to sleep with it still coming down on your head? No fun."

He was going to ask why Goran had done such a thing—why not find shelter somewhere and wait out the storm?—but Goran had wandered off the road and was looking for a reasonable place to bed down. He chose a spot that seemed pretty much identical to the other zillion square miles of nothing, and he sat down.

Mike sat beside him. He had a little food left over from lunch: dry brown bread, a couple tiny hard apples, a lump of something alleging to be cheese. He silently split the meager morsels in half and gave Goran his share. They chewed and swallowed without complaint and washed it all down with a few gulps from a water skin Goran had acquired. When dusk fell, they lay on their backs and looked up at the sky.

"That's mine," Goran said after a while, pointing off to the right a little.

"Your what?"

Goran turned his head to look at Mike. "My constellation. Goran the Hunter. Don't you know the story?"

"No, sorry."

"My parents used to tell it to me when I was very small. Tomismoran, the king of the gods, made humans one day when he was bored. But after a while he lost interest, and the people began to starve. But one of them—Goran—learned to hunt. He could take down game from so far away that anyone else would only see a speck on the horizon. He fed his people and showed them how to hunt too."

"A hero."

Goran's teeth glittered in the starlight when he smiled. "Yes. But everyone kept telling him how wonderful he was, and I guess after a while, it went to his head. He claimed even the gods couldn't hunt as well as him—not even Tomismoran."

Mike had been subjected to enough Greek and Roman mythology to know that was a bad idea. "What happened?"

"Tomismoran struck him through the heart with an arrow. See it? Those stars over there."

Mike just saw random stars, but didn't say so. "That's harsh."

"Goran should have remembered his place. The gods set him in the sky as a reminder to all people that we are only human."

"So he was like one of those celebrities who starts believing all the stuff the fans say. Probably an easy trap to fall into. He was still a hero for saving everyone, wasn't he?"

Goran's smile widened. "Yes." And then he scanned the sky and asked, "Which stars are yours, Mike?"

The stars were different here. Mike didn't know much about the constellations even at home, but at least there he could pick out the two

Dippers. Here there was only a chaos of tiny faraway lights. "I don't have any."

Now Goran propped himself up on one elbow. "You don't? Then who are you named after?"

"Um, nobody. My parents just liked the name." He didn't mention his middle name, which he'd inherited from his father's grandfather.

"Hmm." Goran collapsed onto his back again. "If there's no story already about Mike, I think we should create one. Let's see… Mike the Traveler. He charmed even goddesses with his pretty face—"

"I am *not* pretty!"

"Oh, I wasn't talking about *you*. I meant him." Goran pointed to the sky. "That Mike. He had a pretty face and he chatted with gods. And he traveled very far, but eventually he came home again with… with pockets full of gold and enough stories to fill a hundred books. He was very popular."

Mike snorted. "Well, definitely not me, then."

"Three dozen new suitors showed up at his door every single day, every one of them madly in love with the pretty, rich adventurer. One day Mike fell in love with one of them too, and they got married."

"And lived happily ever after?"

"Yes. Because Mike the Traveler was much smarter than Goran the Hunter and knew not to anger any gods."

Shaking his head, Mike said, "If Mike's so smart, he should know there's no such thing as love and happily ever after."

There was a momentary pause. "You don't believe in love?" Goran sounded unbelieving and a little sad.

"It makes a good story."

Mike turned his back to Goran and closed his eyes. After a moment or two, he heard Goran shuffling around on the ground a bit, trying to make himself comfortable. Soft snores soon followed.

But even though he was exhausted, Mike didn't fall asleep. He kept thinking about the way he had felt with Goran's arm around him and the sound of Goran's soft chuckle in the darkness as he told his silly tale about Mike the Traveler. A tale he'd given a happier ending than Goran the Hunter had earned.

Moving as slowly and quietly as possible, Mike rolled over to face Goran. Who, as it turned out, was facing him. But Goran's eyes were closed, his mouth hanging slightly open. A few strands of hair had escaped the leather tie and lay across one cheek. One of his hands was curled softly near his face, and in the moonlight he looked much younger—a boy with several days' growth of whiskers. He looked strangely vulnerable too, which was stupid because, as always, he wore his weapons and could no doubt handily slice and dice anything that threatened him.

Mike had underestimated him at first. Goran might be uneducated, but he was a lot brighter than Mike had originally given him credit for. He liked his alcohol a bit too much, but he was kind. And although he grinned often and had an easy laugh, there were depths of sorrow to him. He claimed to have no family—although he'd admitted he'd once had parents who told him about his namesake—and he never mentioned friends.

And he was beautiful. God, he was so beautiful.

Mike didn't realize he'd slipped his hand under his waistband until he felt his cock hardening beneath his palm. Flushing hotly, he rolled away from Goran. But he didn't move his hand away. Instead, he began to stroke himself.

He tried very hard not to remember what had happened last time he attempted to jerk off. He didn't want any demanding gods showing up right now. Instead, he closed his eyes and bit his lower lip, and he thought about Goran. He felt a little guilty about it—beating off to fantasies of a man who lay right beside him—but although he tried to imagine past bed partners or porn stars or even a couple of his favorite actors, it was Goran who filled his mind.

In surprisingly little time, Mike's cock and hand were slick with precome and his balls were tingling. He wished he could have kicked off his filthy clothing. He wished he was on a soft mattress instead of the hard ground. Christ, he wished someone else's hand was gripping him, twisting just so, moving just like *that*.

Mike came with a muffled grunt.

He had no way to clean his hand, his dick and belly, his clothes. So he fell asleep like that, dirty and empty.

Chapter 7

THE UPHILL climb was long and steep. Mike's feet had become accustomed to the sandals by now, and his legs had stopped aching. His body had given up complaining about his stony beds. But his stomach still demanded food, and Goran's water skin provided too little liquid for them both.

"It'll be better soon," Goran said, making an obvious attempt to cheer him. "The rain falls on that side of the mountain, so the land is more fertile. There are more people too. We'll pass through a real town."

"Good. Maybe someone will know what I'm supposed to do at the shrine in Ugolin."

"And we can find food and ale."

"Of course *and ale*." Mike carefully didn't look at Goran when he asked the next question. "Why do you drink so much?"

Goran shrugged. "I'm thirsty."

"But you get drunk whenever you can."

"Whenever I can, as long as I can. When you pay me, I'll have enough money to stay drunk for months."

They reached a spot where they had to clamber up rocks using their hands to keep from slipping backward in the scree. Mike carefully avoided looking to the left, where a sheer drop-off scared the crap out of him. He'd never been very fond of heights. "Why are you so interested in staying drunk?" he asked a little breathlessly.

"What else is there?"

"I don't know. Work?"

Goran snorted. "I work to have enough money for ale."

Fair enough. "What about family?"

"I told you. I have no family."

"But you *could*. You could meet someone and—"

"No." Goran's voice was hard, and although Mike couldn't see his face—Goran was behind him—he could imagine it was set in anger. It occurred to Mike that his companion was potentially as dangerous as the mountain they now navigated.

But then they reached a relatively level spot where the road widened enough for them to walk side by side for a short time. Goran gave Mike's shoulder a quick squeeze. "I'm not like you, Mike. Soft. And I don't mean that as an insult. I only mean—you see that bit of moss over there, under that rock? It's soft to the touch and it's growing, changing. If we came by here in a few weeks, it wouldn't look the same. But me, I'm the rock. The only way it can change is if it's broken."

Mike wasn't sure he fully understood the analogy. And he wasn't any closer to learning what had hardened Goran, stolen his family, driven him to drink. None of his business, Mike supposed. He'd hired the guy to guide him; that didn't mean Mike got to psychoanalyze him. Hell, Mike had a couple of pretty big skeletons in his closet too. He sighed, and then was almost happy for the distraction of another dangerous stretch of pathway.

GORAN WAS right—the other side of the mountain was better. Even though they were still high on the slope, plants grew lushly, and small animals scuttled through the brush. Goran threw a rock at a large rodent thing hard enough to kill it. Mike would have felt sorry for the beast, which resembled an oversized squirrel with a thin, striped tail. But he was hungry, and it took Goran mere minutes to skin and clean the animal, start a fire, and set it to cooking.

"Keep it from burning," Goran ordered.

"Why? Where are you going?"

"To find water."

Mike took a seat on the springy ground near the fire. He watched the fat sizzle and pop in the flames and focused on the pleasure of a decent meal. He had to laugh at how drastically his definition of a decent meal had changed.

He heard Goran return before he saw him, loudly singing a sprightly tune about maidens in spring. Mike twisted around as Goran appeared through some bushes. "Did you find water?"

Goran grinned. "Yes! And even better than that." He held up a red-stained hand. For a heart-stopping moment, Mike thought it was fresh blood. But then he saw that Goran was holding something small between his thumb and forefinger. A berry.

After sitting heavily beside Mike, Goran dumped a handful of fruit onto the leaves in front of him. "I thought it might be too early in the season, but I found a few ripe ones. Go ahead and eat them. I've had my share." He smiled again, revealing slightly reddened teeth.

Mike didn't recognize the berries. They were reminiscent of extra-large currants but were a deeper red, more like cranberries. There weren't many of them, but they tasted delicious: sweet and a little tart. He gobbled them quickly.

"They were my favorites when I was a boy," Goran said. "The first treats of the spring. My mother would send me out to gather them, and then she'd pretend to be angry when I ate half of them before I even got home. She called me her little bundabeast because the bundabeasts like them so much."

He shook himself slightly and tossed the water skin to Mike. "Here. I think our meal's nearly done."

THEY SLEPT on the mountain that night. The ground was soft with a thick layer of pine needles. Just as they were settling down, a doe and her fawn passed close by, making both men smile. "Agata is busy this time of year," Goran said.

"I guess so."

"Maybe that's why she came to you now. Her powers are strongest in spring, and Alina's at her weakest."

"That makes sense." Mike rearranged his makeshift bed a little, then yawned. "I was born the first day of spring. March twenty-first."

"Spring begins the first day of Dvor for us. But either way, it's a lucky day to be born."

"When's your birthday?"

"I don't know. Sometime in the summer. My mother told me I was born on an unusually hot day." Goran chuckled lightly. "I'm not sure she ever quite forgave me for that."

Minutes later, he was snoring. Mike didn't jack off. The forest canopy blocked any glow from the night sky, so he couldn't make out Goran's face.

The next morning, they were soon off the mountain, walking through gently rolling farmland. Mike could tell at once that the people here were more prosperous, although they still worked very hard. They seemed surprised to see Mike and Goran. Probably few travelers made their way over the mountain.

They reached the town by noon. "Market day," Goran observed as crowds of people swarmed around them, many heading to and from the center square, which reminded Mike of a modern county fair but with medieval trappings. People sold produce, meat, and live animals as well as fabric, tools, kitchen implements, and other items he couldn't identify. There was cooked food too, and just like at the modern fair, a lot of it seemed to come on sticks. However, Mike had never attended a fair that served giant crickets, roasted and salted.

"Bug kebab. Ugh."

Goran looked at him like he was nuts. Certainly the locals were enjoying the treat—the cricket stand had gathered an eager crowd. Still, Mike was relieved when Goran kept walking through the market, leading him down a series of progressively narrower streets. Goran stopped in front of an open doorway where a thin man in a stained apron was leaning, watching them. The sign above the door bore a crude painting of a goblet and something that looked like a lumpy turkey leg.

"My master is a pilgrim," Goran said to the man without preamble. "He's journeyed very far already. Can you spare us food and ale?"

The man narrowed his eyes. "Going to Ugolin?"

"Yes."

"Tell that old bitch Alina I'm not afraid of her."

Goran nodded slightly.

They didn't enter the inn, but the man ducked inside. He returned shortly with clay tankards and plates heaped with food. There was a grain something like rice but nuttier and slivers of meat and vegetables. Goran demonstrated how to use a thin tortilla-like bread to scoop everything up and into the mouth. They squatted outside the inn while they ate. Mike had long since given up caring about hygiene.

Mike drank only the single tankard of ale, which was plenty. But the innkeeper refilled Goran's cup three times, never saying a word. It was a strange sort of generosity, thin-lipped and grim.

"Thank you," Goran said to the man when their meal was done.

The innkeeper glared. "You make sure and tell her. Miho at the Spotted Horse isn't afraid of her!"

"We'll tell her."

"She's shown me her worst already, she has. Took my wife, all my children except the oldest, and he's the laziest sod that ever set foot on this earth. She can't hurt me." He spat on the cobblestones and turned to reenter his inn.

"Excuse me!" Mike called.

Miho paused and swiveled his head. "Gave you enough already."

"It was very kind of you. I just had a question, actually. I'm not sure… what am I supposed to offer her at the Ugolin shrine?"

The smile Miho gave him in return was the least cheery expression Mike had ever seen. "Gotta give the bitch blood," Miho said. And then he went inside.

UGOLIN TURNED out to be a village a couple hours' walk from the city—sort of a suburb, Mike thought. It was a pretty little place whose well-kept wooden houses sprouted window boxes full of flowers. There weren't many people around—Goran explained that those who weren't out working the fields were likely at the market in town—but a few older folks stared at them from doorways. One whole section of the village consisted of workshops, all of them abandoned for the day. Metalsmiths, Goran said. The village was known for them.

Just past the village, a narrow pathway twisted through a flower-speckled meadow and skirted a small hillock before passing under an elaborate iron archway. Mike thought this was strange, because there was no wall or fence, just the arch. Once he was through the archway, he saw hundreds of small metal bowls with lids. They were laid out in careful rows, and the vegetation between each row had been flattened by trampling feet.

"What is this place?" Mike asked, looking around in bewilderment.

"Garden of the dead." Goran's mood was unusually somber despite the fact that he still swayed a bit from the ale.

"Garden of— You mean it's a cemetery?"

"It's where the ashes of the dead are kept."

Weird. Although once Mike thought it through, it wasn't any weirder than preserving corpses, sticking them in expensive boxes, and burying them. "The shrine is here somewhere?"

Goran wordlessly gestured at an extra-large bowl near one corner of the garden. It was big enough for Mike to sit in, if he wanted to, and it had no lid. When he drew closer, he saw that the insides of the bowl were badly stained. His stomach lurched. Blood. He startled when Goran set a hand on his shoulder.

"I'll go get an animal. Shouldn't take long." He pointed at a small stand of trees near the garden. "I'll find something there."

"An animal? To kill, you mean?"

"You heard the innkeeper. You need a blood offering."

"But… I don't want to *kill* something."

Goran shrugged. "I'll kill it for you. You've seen already—I'm good at it. It's what I was made for." He sounded bitter. He turned to walk away, but Mike caught his arm.

"Don't," Mike said. It didn't seem right that some poor creature had to die. True, Mike was no vegetarian. He'd eaten meat twice already that day. But there was a difference between killing to survive and killing just to soothe some god's hurt feelings. He didn't think he could explain this to Goran, though, because he barely understood it himself. "Just give me your knife," he said with a sigh.

"You'll offer your own blood?"

"Yeah. I mean, I don't plan to exsanguinate myself or anything. Just... I don't know. A couple ounces or so. Do you think that's enough?"

"I don't know." Goran drew his knife from the sheath and handed it over. But while Mike was still trying to decide where to maim himself, Goran held up a hand. "Wait! Not yet." He spun around and sprinted away.

"Don't kill anything!" Mike called after him. He felt stupid just standing there, so while he waited, he strolled around the garden, looking at the lidded bowls. Although all were about the same size and shape, each bowl was uniquely decorated with raised designs. Some of the designs were just abstract shapes and some were stylized leaves and flowers, but others looked like dogs or campfires or wheeled carts. Some showed faceless people sewing, tending to faceless babies, harvesting food. Quite a few were faceless men working at forges. And several of the bowls included couples—both het and gay—engaged in various sexual acts.

Goran came running back into the garden with something clenched in his hands. "I'm ready now," he said a little breathlessly.

Together they walked to the shrine. Mike folded back his left sleeve, wincing at the grime seemingly embedded in his skin. He took the water skin from around Goran's waist, wet his forearm, scrubbed a bit, and rinsed. And then he sliced himself crosswise.

The blade was very keen. Goran had a sharpening stone that he used often, making sure his knife and sword were finely honed. He'd even lectured Mike about it, saying that sometimes the difference between life and death was the sharpness of a man's blade. So now Mike barely felt the cut at all. Holding the knife handle in his right hand, he positioned his bleeding arm over the giant bowl. He and Goran both watched as the thick red liquid pattered against the metal with a distinct ping-ping.

"That's enough," Goran said gently. He took Mike's hand and turned his arm over as he pulled it away from the bowl. The bleeding had already begun to slow. But then Goran smushed his other hand over the cut, pressing hard with a bunch of sharp-smelling leaves.

"Ow!" Mike protested, trying to pull away. "That really stings."

Goran hung on to him. "Stay still. It's marrowweed. Helps with healing and stops infection."

Mike stopped struggling. "Oh."

"It's not as good as dragontail, but it's the wrong time of year for that. Marrowweed should do well enough. I've used it many times."

"*Dragon* tail? You have dragons?" Mike couldn't stop a nervous glance upward, as if a fire-breathing serpent might be circling overhead.

Goran laughed. "Don't be ridiculous! There's no such thing as dragons. The stems are thick and sort of scaly, so I suppose someone thought they looked like a dragon's tail might. It's an ugly plant, but the sap is very useful for wounds. But as I said, it's too early in the season."

Mike nodded. He felt a little silly for asking about dragons. But really, were they any less likely than universe-hopping and gods who appeared in the flesh while you were in the middle of jerking off?

After instructing Mike to hold the leaves in place, Goran tore a strip of cloth from the hem of Mike's shirt. He tied the cloth firmly around Mike's arm, keeping the marrowweed in place. "You should have some blackflower tea too. I'll see if I can find some when we're back on the road."

"Okay. You, um, seem to know a fair bit about healing." Apparently literacy was rare around here, but perhaps these people had mandatory first-aid courses.

"I've learned a few things," said Goran. He didn't look happy about it, which was strange. He took the dagger back, wiped it very carefully on some broad leaves, and slipped it back into the sheath.

Mike improvised another quick prayer to Alina and then conveyed Miho's message in somewhat less disrespectful terms. Together, he and Goran left the garden of death.

Chapter 8

THEY STOPPED for the night somewhat earlier than usual. That was partly because Mike's arm was throbbing painfully, and Goran wanted to change the dressing and give him some tea. In addition, Mike wanted to read the next section of the book to see where they should go next. Besides, by early evening they'd entered a thick forest, and little of the remaining light filtered through the leaves.

Goran fussed over Mike. He found him a comfortable spot to sit where the ground was soft from decomposing leaves and Mike could lean against the trunk of a huge tree. Then Goran lit a fire. He'd begged a tin pot and a clay mug from an old woman in the city of smiths. The pot had a broken handle, but he was able to prop it over the fire and fill it with water he'd collected from a small stream. He sprinkled some plants into the pot, and as he waited for the water to heat, he checked Mike's arm.

"It doesn't look inflamed," Goran said. "That's good."

Mike smiled at him. "The marrowweed must have helped."

"You still need to drink the tea. And eat. I'll catch us something." He frowned sternly. "Don't tell me not to. You need meat."

Deciding to ignore the double entendre, Mike said, "That's fine. You go bash out the brains of some adorable furry thing, and I'll scarf it down. I just didn't want something to die so that I could make an offering."

Goran gave him an odd look before packing some fresh leaves onto the wound and retying the makeshift bandage. He must have judged the water sufficiently heated, because he poured it into the mug. "Drink this," he ordered, handing it to Mike.

The first sip burned his tongue and tasted like bong water. He made a face.

"Drink it *all*," Goran scolded. "If you end up with gangrene and I have to amputate your arm, that's really going to slow down our journey."

"Gee. Thanks for the kind thoughts."

Goran grinned and ruffled Mike's already tangled hair. "Back soon." Then he disappeared into the trees.

Mike pulled out his book and read by firelight as he choked down the entire mug of tea. Maybe it was only psychosomatic, but his arm felt better when he was done. He remembered the liquid antiseptic his mother used to pour on his childhood cuts and scrapes. He always complained, but she just applied more. "If it's stinging, that means it's working," she'd say. He wondered whether his mother and Goran would get along. Mom would probably think Goran's hair was too long—she was forever nagging Mike about haircuts when he was a kid—but she'd be impressed by his good looks and Eagle Scout-like skills. And she'd probably enjoy the way he sang all the time when he was happy. Mike had inherited his lack of musical ability from his father. Mom sang pretty well.

Jesus. Mike's mother was never going to meet Goran. She was literally worlds away. Mike would be very lucky if he ever saw her again himself.

Goran returned before long. This time he carried something that looked like a cross between a pigeon and an alligator. "We're supposed to eat that?" Mike asked.

"You've never had marblebird? They're ugly but tasty." Goran sat a little way from the fire and began plucking the thing. "And they're stupid. Really easy to kill. They're one of the first things I hunted." His big hands moved deftly, confidently.

"I drank all the tea. Thank you."

"Good boy," Goran said with a grin. "I'll let you eat the liver."

"Ugh. And I'm not a boy."

For a while they were silent, Goran working and Mike watching him through the flickering flames. Insects chirped and trilled, an owl hooted, and a light breeze set the overhead leaves whispering. The air smelled really good, Mike noticed. Fresh, like young growing things. He was sleepy, but pleasantly so, not the end-of-the-day exhaustion he'd been experiencing lately. Maybe the tea had something to do with that, or maybe it was just watching a handsome man look at him and smile every few moments.

"That was an interesting choice," Goran said softly when he finished preparing the bird. He stood, moved closer to the fire, and propped the carcass over the flames.

"What was?"

"Offering your own blood. It was... kind of you." His back was to Mike, so Mike couldn't see his expression.

"I don't know. I guess it was kind of silly. I'm fainthearted."

Goran turned to look at him. "A fainthearted man doesn't willingly slice into his own flesh. And it wasn't silly." He squinted thoughtfully. "You are a kind man, aren't you?"

Mike snorted. "Hardly. I'm a selfish sonofabitch." It was true. He'd never gone out of his way to harm others, but he almost always put his own needs and desires above everyone else's. He didn't donate much to charity, and when he did, he always took the tax deduction. He didn't volunteer his time anywhere. When he was near people who held cardboard signs begging for food or money or a job, he pretended he didn't see them.

In fact, he'd been called coldhearted. That was what Benny had called him the night he'd dumped Mike for the guy he'd been screwing on the side. "I can't try with you anymore!" Benny had yelled. "You just won't let me in, dammit. You won't let anyone in. You keep yourself locked up like a fucking bank vault. I need more. *Everyone* needs more. You better learn to open up or you're always gonna wake up alone."

"Are you all right, Mike? Is your arm hurting?"

Mike blinked and again focused on Goran. "No, it's fine. I was just woolgathering."

"Didn't look like you were enjoying it much." Goran sat next to him, almost close enough that they were touching, and leaned back against the tree to watch the marblebird cook. "Did you find out where we're going next?"

"Varesh?"

"Really? You do realize that your book is leading us in a roundabout way, don't you? We'll have to backtrack south again almost to the border."

"Sorry. There's no map or anything. The author did say something about labyrinths making for better penitents, but I didn't really understand that part. He spouts off about all kinds of stuff, and most of it doesn't seem to have much to do with being a pilgrim."

"It's fine." Goran seemed to consider for a few moments. "Actually, if you don't mind, I'm going to take us on a longer route to Varesh. It'll add several days to the trip, but we'll get to spend almost the whole time in the forest. Otherwise we're going to have to climb Demon's Tooth, and it's nastier than the mountain we already crossed."

Demon's Tooth? Not without proper hiking boots and a shopping trip at REI. "Forest it is."

"Good. It reminds me of ho—the place I lived when I was a child."

"There were a lot of woods where you grew up?" Mike asked cautiously. He didn't want to scare Goran away from talking about his family again.

But Goran nodded as he stared into the fire. "Yes. Most people there farmed, but not us. My father was the lord's lead huntsman. He caught game for the lord's household. Father taught me the bow and sling, but it was my mother who showed me how to use a sword. She was deadly with hers. I was nearly born with a weapon in my hands. I was hunting almost before I could walk."

"Now I understand why your parents named you Goran."

"It was more apt than they knew," Goran said bleakly. He stood and disappeared quickly into the forest. He didn't show up again until the bird was ready to eat.

The marblebird *was* tasty. Mike admitted as much to Goran, who gave him a weak smile. But then Goran perked up a little when Mike obediently drank more of that vile tea. They made their quick bedtime preparations and slept within arm's reach of each other, lit by the slight glow of the dying coals.

MIKE DECIDED he liked the forest. There were no towns at all, which meant Goran had to hunt and gather everything they ate. But he was good at it, and they ate well. He even taught Mike how to search for some sweet purple berries and showed him how the young leaves of a certain tree were tasty, if slightly tough. You had to chew them thoroughly. There was no alcohol either, which was a good thing. More of Goran's true self showed through when he wasn't drunk—and Mike was learning how much he liked Goran's true self.

The road through the forest was soft and comfortable under Mike's feet. The daytime temperatures were perfect, and although the nights were chilly, the travelers easily found wood for a fire. Interesting-looking plants grew among the trees, and birds and animals were everywhere once Mike learned how to look for them. He wasn't as keen about the bugs, however; this world had voracious mosquitos and spiders as big as saucers.

He liked the quiet. It was a different sort of quiet than he'd experienced before. Even when he was home alone, he usually had the TV on or music playing, or he'd watch videos online. And of course he couldn't escape the sound of traffic, noisy neighbors, low-flying airplanes. He learned that he could walk beside Goran for hours with neither of them saying a word, and yet there was nothing awkward about it. Sometimes they exchanged smiles over nothing at all.

But Mike discovered the best thing about the forest several days in, when the trees unexpectedly thinned and he and Goran found themselves beside a clear spring-fed pond. "Would you like to bathe?" asked Goran, who'd probably grown tired of hearing Mike whine about being filthy and stinky.

"God, yes! And can we wash our clothes?"

"If you like. We'll have to camp here, though, unless you want to walk in wet clothing."

It was only about noon, but Mike nodded eagerly. He was ready to sacrifice a half day of travel if it meant being temporarily clean again.

They ate first—some leftover game from breakfast, along with a handful of sweetish tubers Goran had collected and roasted the night before. Mike was so eager to get into the water that he gobbled quickly, making Goran laugh.

But Goran ate fast too, so they finished about the same time. Goran stripped first, unbuckling his belt and setting it gently on a boulder near the water's edge. It was one of the few times Mike had seen him unarmed. Then Goran unlaced his boots and kicked them off. He didn't wear socks. But when he pulled off his tunic, Mike almost forgot to breathe.

He'd known Goran was magnificent—the tunic was tight enough to leave little to the imagination. But to actually see those bulging biceps, the powerful chest covered in dark hairs, the line of hair that trailed down Goran's flat belly to the waistband of his trousers… trousers that he was now tugging past his muscular, hairy thighs and then completely off. His uncut cock was thick and soft, his balls heavy but not too pendulous, and the whole package nestled in a luxuriant bush of dark curls.

Mike was unaware that he'd frozen in place and was staring until Goran gave him an angry glare, turned quickly—flashing a backside at least as spectacular as the front—and dove into the pond with a huge splash.

It took much longer for Mike to undress. Not because his clothes were more numerous or more complicated, but because he was suddenly self-conscious. He'd been in relatively decent shape before this little adventure, and all the days of limited food and steady walking had worked off the couple of extra pounds he'd been carrying. But he was… lean. In a really good mood, he might claim lithe. And he was perfectly averagely endowed. But Goran was spectacular, like the statue of a Greek demigod brought to life. He was majestic and luscious and jaw-dropping and—

"What's *that*?"

Mike glanced nervously down at himself. He'd taken off everything except his blue briefs, which after many days of constant use were now considerably worse for wear. "My underwear," Mike answered.

Goran stood hip-deep in the water, staring. "What? They're... tiny trousers. And very tight."

"They're underwear. In California we wear them under our clothes." Well, most people did, anyway. He'd hooked up with more than one guy who went commando.

"Why?" Goran cocked his head like a curious puppy.

"Um... cleanliness, I guess."

"They don't look very clean."

"They're not. They're gross. But if I were back home, I'd have a bunch of pairs and do my laundry regularly so I could put on a clean pair every day."

"That's odd. Your people have a strange obsession with cleanliness, don't they? And why is there writing on it? Is it your name?"

Mike looked at the waistband. "It's the name of the company that makes them." They'd been a birthday gift from his mother, which was way too embarrassing to admit.

Goran was still bewildered, scratching his short wet beard as he thought. "Why is that necessary?"

"Advertisement, I guess." When he was met with a blank look, Mike added, "So people will see it and want some of their own."

"But how will they see it if it's under your clothes?"

"I... I don't know." Mike skimmed off the puzzling article of clothing and quickly plunged into the water. His balls instantly attempted to tunnel into his body. "C-cold!" he exclaimed when he came up for air. Goran laughed and splashed him.

They spent a few minutes paddling around. Once Mike got used to the temperature, the water felt wonderful. The last time he'd gone skinny-dipping, he was four years old and playing in one of those blue plastic pools. This was nice. He felt much lighter, as much from the grime washing away as from the buoyancy of the water.

Dripping and shivering, he hurried out of the pond to fetch the lump of soap he'd bought at the beginning of the journey. He took it back to the water. It wasn't very sudsy and it smelled a little like steak, but with some dedicated rubbing, it did a reasonable enough job of removing the dirt. Mike used it as a makeshift shampoo too. God, it felt so *good* to have clean hair!

When Mike was finished with the soap, he handed it to Goran and then couldn't stop himself from watching as Goran scrubbed. Goran was beautiful even when he was dirty, but clean, with his long dark hair hanging down his back and water running in rivulets down his pecs and belly, over his groin and thighs…. The pond water was not cold enough to discourage Mike's cock. He stayed as deeply submerged as possible so Goran wouldn't see his hard-on.

"Do you want to clean your clothing now?" Goran asked, holding out the diminished lump of soap.

"You go ahead. I'll wait."

Which meant Mike got to watch Goran emerge from the pond and then squat at the edge of the water to scour his trousers and tunic. The process took considerable time and did nothing to deflate Mike's raging erection. After Goran spread his clothing on a sunny patch of boulder, he turned to Mike's things.

"You don't have to do that for me," Mike said as he treaded water.

"Consider it an extra service."

Oh, Mike was considering extra services all right. He ducked his head briefly underwater in a vain attempt to cool off.

Goran worked on Mike's trousers and tunic first and then picked up the briefs. He turned them curiously in his hands, making Mike's cheeks burn. "Look, Goran, you don't have to—"

"Is it so your lovers can see who made your underwear?"

"Um, maybe."

"Do your lovers approve of this maker?"

Why the hell was Goran so fascinated with the damn things? "I have no idea. I haven't had a lover in a while."

"Oh." Goran made no move to begin washing the things. He stood at the edge of the water, naked and glorious, lost in thought. Finally he looked over at Mike. "You're the first person to see me without clothes in… in a long time."

There was something strangely tentative about Goran's statement, as if he feared the response. So Mike kept his voice even when he replied. "Why?"

Goran traced a long mark that ran from beneath his ribcage to his side, then one crosswise on his left thigh, and another atop the left shoulder. He ran a finger over his right pec too. Goran's chest hair was thick, and Mike was too far away to see, but he assumed another mark there.

"Scars?" asked Mike.

"They're ugly. I…. People stare at me, like you did when I first undressed. Disgusted."

Mike was so flabbergasted he took a few moments to find words. "I didn't…. Jesus, Goran, I was *not* staring out of disgust. I barely even noticed the scars until you pointed them out." That was true. He'd seen them, of course, but they'd hardly registered because he was so overcome by Goran's overall magnificence.

"But you *were* staring. I saw you."

"I…. Do you have any idea what you look like?" Mike had to ask, because the only mirror he'd seen in this world was the reflective surface of the pond before they'd hopped in.

Goran shrugged. "Big. I'm not so young anymore. Scars everywhere."

"You're the most beautiful man I've ever seen," Mike said.

That made Goran blink. "Either the men in your country are ugly or you're teasing me."

"Oh, for fuck's sake!" Mike splashed inelegantly toward the shore. He stopped when the water came to midthigh, revealing his bobbing hard-on. He gestured at his crotch. "Does *this* look like I'm lying?"

Goran's mouth split into a huge and delighted grin—and, Mike couldn't help but notice, Goran's cock jerked a little too. "You find me attractive?" Goran said. He sounded absurdly like an insecure teenage girl.

"I find you extremely attractive," Mike said firmly. And then, slightly mortified over the entire exchange, he turned and headed back to deeper water.

Goran wasn't mortified at all. In fact, he seemed very happy, humming and singing as he washed Mike's briefs. As he worked, he kept flashing smiles in Mike's direction. Mike decided the humiliation had been worth it.

After Goran was through with the laundry, he lay down on a springy spot of grass and moss, offering himself to the sun. Mike swam for a while but eventually got out. When he did, Goran leaned up on an elbow and smiled. "Do you feel better now?"

"Much." Then Mike reached up to rub his cheek. "Wish I had a razor, though."

"I can shave you if you like. I was going to scrape my own beard away."

"Using what?"

"My knife, of course," Goran replied with a chuckle. He hopped to his feet, walked over to his belt, and bent to retrieve the weapon— giving Mike a mouthwatering view of his upraised ass. Mike suspected he might be doing it on purpose. Mike's hard-on might have made a return appearance, except Goran was waving his very large, sharp blade.

Mike swallowed. "Um, I don't know."

"If I wanted to slit your throat, I would have done it a long time ago. Come on, Mike. Trust me."

Oddly enough, Mike *did* trust him. Out of necessity, Mike had put more faith in Goran than he had in anyone from his previous life, and Goran hadn't let him down. So even though his legs felt a little shaky, he walked to the large smooth rock Goran was pointing at and he sat. The sun-warmed stone felt nice under his water-chilled ass.

Now he wasn't sure what made him more uneasy: the nearness of that knife to his neck or the nearness of Goran's bare belly to his face. He tried to remain statue-still, and he concentrated on Goran's scars, which were now very evident. There were a lot of them—not just the large ones Goran had pointed out, but many small ones. Most looked to be the result of straight cuts, although a few were irregular. He found himself wanting to touch them as badly as he wanted to run his fingers through Goran's body hair and stroke the big, soft cock.

Goran handled him firmly but gently, turning Mike's head this way and that as he manipulated the blade over vulnerable skin. It was more intimate than any sex Mike had experienced for a very long time, although it wasn't precisely sexual. Goran frowned with concentration as he worked, and just the very tip of his tongue stuck out from his full lips.

"You have so many colors in your hair," Goran said softly, scraping the knife along Mike's jawline. "Yellow and red and brown. Pretty, just like the rest of you."

Mike wanted to protest again that he wasn't pretty, but he decided that arguing with the man wielding a dagger close to his Adam's apple was unwise.

Goran squinted at him and then, nodding with satisfaction, moved to the other side of the rock to work on the rest of Mike's face. "I used to shave Pavo like this. My husband. But his hair was almost as dark as mine."

Hoping Goran would reveal a few more hints of his past, Mike made a noncommittal noise. He was relieved when Goran gave a small smile. "Pavo always had trouble sitting still for so long. He was always in motion, even when we were both hardly more than babies."

"So you knew him a long time?"

"Since I was born. He lived in the castle. His father was our lord's head groom, and they had a room over the stables. My family lived just outside the castle in the lord's woods, and whenever one of us could get away from work, we'd run to find the other." He grinned. "Pavo escaped more often. He was very fast. His father would yell for him, and we'd only laugh and run faster."

"He... sounds like a good friend."

"I loved him. Always. Always knew we'd marry, even when we were very young. My mother would get angry when I told her so because she wanted grandchildren, but his parents didn't seem to mind. They had a big family."

Goran still shaved Mike, but his movements had grown very slow and his voice sounded far away. "When I was ten years old, my father sent us deep into the woods and told us not to return until we had enough meat to feed us for a month. He told me to teach Pavo to hunt, but we all knew Pavo wouldn't learn. He missed on purpose. He was like you—kindhearted. Didn't want to kill anything."

"Ten seems young to be in the woods alone."

"I knew those woods well. I'd been hunting in them for years already. I think… I'm fairly certain my father knew what would happen. Even I had heard the talk, although I was too young to truly understand it, and I'd seen the lord's men preparing their weapons." By now, Goran had stopped his work entirely. The knife hung at his side, forgotten. "Our lord was in a dispute with the neighboring lord, who was much more powerful."

Mike's stomach clenched uncomfortably. Much as he wanted to know more about Goran, he was a little tempted to shut him up. He knew the rest of this tale wouldn't be happy.

But Mike said nothing, and Goran continued, quietly and slowly. "Yes, Father knew. But Mother had died that spring, and her new son along with her, and since then Father had cared about very little except drinking. And me. He still loved me. He sent me and Pavo deep into the forest and told us not to come back for a while. We were thrilled. Days with no adult supervision, no chores. We had a wonderful time.

"But eventually we had to return home. Only, when we did… home was gone. The castle was in ruins, parts of it still burning. Death was everywhere. Pavo's parents and siblings had tried to hide above the stable, but they'd been killed. Even the baby. I found my father just outside our little hut. He'd been run straight through the heart with a sword. He wasn't even armed." Goran laughed without humor. "My father the huntsman had lifted no weapon against the attackers."

There were no words of solace for a loss like that, even if it had been long ago. Mike patted Goran's arm instead, which seemed to bring Goran back to himself. "I'm sorry," Goran said. "I didn't mean—"

"What did you do? You and Pavo?"

"We left. There was nothing more for us there. I suppose we could have stayed in the woods awhile, but we didn't know where the other lord's men were. Perhaps now they'd use the forest to hunt. So we gathered a few things and we left. We walked for… a very long time, until we came to a city. Strazha. Neither of us had ever been more than a few hours from the castle. We didn't really know how to live in a place like that. Pavo was smart, though. Like you. He found us ways to survive. And we grew up and married, just as we'd always planned."

Goran shook his head and again grasped Mike's head. He returned to his task. Mike waited until Goran was finished, then stood and ran a hand over his cheeks. "Thank you. That feels much better. You make a good barber." He briefly squeezed Goran's shoulder.

Although Goran's eyes were still filled with sorrow, he managed a small smile. "It's a shame to hide that pretty face behind a beard."

Mike smiled back at him.

A few minutes later, it was Mike's turn to warm himself on the bank of the pond while Goran shaved. Mike had thought him very handsome with a beard, but with the whiskers gone he was truly stunning. He had a firm, dimpled chin, just like a Harlequin cover model. It was scarred as well, but the scar added character. Without it, his face would have been almost *too* perfect.

After cleaning his blade and returning it to the sheath, Goran flopped down beside Mike. They stared at the cloud-dotted sky, at a few passing birds. "I wish we could just stay here," Mike admitted after a while.

"We can, if you like. You're the master and I'm not in such a hurry."

Mike thought of angry gods, of his mother and sister back home, frantic and grieving. "No. I have to get back."

"To Calif… Calif…."

"California. Yes."

"And your clean underwear with the words on it."

"Yes," Mike said with a laugh. "Back to that. And… other things. You know, I'm pretty useless here, but back home I'm good at a lot of things. Parallel parking. Tax returns. I can wrangle the ugliest spreadsheet into submission. I can name every World Series winner going back to 1978. I can find *anything* on Google."

"I don't know what any of that means."

"I know. But it's all very useful back home. Well, maybe not so much the World Series thing, although I've won a few bar bets that way. But my point is, I'm good at stuff in California. Here I'm… helpless. I'd probably be dead already if it weren't for you."

Goran turned his head to look into Mike's eyes. "You have value here too."

Maybe what happened next was inevitable. They were both naked. Mike had recently and very publicly demonstrated his attraction to Goran, and privately he had jacked off while thinking about him. Neither of them had gotten laid in… a long time in Mike's case, and a couple weeks at least in Goran's. They were both feeling raw and emotional after Goran's story. And there was the touching during the shave, the tender grasping of Mike's face by Goran's calloused fingers.

Almost in unison, they rolled into each other's arms.

Goran smelled like water, soap, sunshine, and crushed herbs. His skin was soft over planes of hard muscle, and Mike buried his fingers in his long, slightly damp hair. Goran tasted good too. He'd taken lately to stealing Mike's tooth-cleaning twigs, and they'd had berries for lunch, so Goran's kiss was sweet. He had plump lips and an agile tongue, and sharp teeth that nipped gently at Mike's ears and jaw and collarbone.

Mike found himself flat on his back with a double handful of Goran's ass while Goran hovered over him like an incubus. Goran's hair hung in curtains, creating a very private space between their faces. His green eyes glittered and sparked. "I want this so badly," he said in a voice hardly more than a moan. "Want you. Please?"

Mike was in no mood to refuse. He gripped those glutes a little more tightly and urged Goran's hips down so their groins pressed together, their hard cocks finding a bit of badly needed friction. Goran groaned loudly. He licked and nibbled on Mike's neck and shoulder before moving down to suck on one hardened nipple and then the other. Mike was already breathing hard, pushing up with his hips as much as he was able.

When Goran left a trail of wet kisses down Mike's sternum and stomach, Mike expected his cock to be next. But instead Goran gently tugged at Mike's arms and repositioned them so that they were spread widely on the ground. Goran snuffled under Mike's left armpit, licked the length of his upper arm, kissed the crook of his elbow.

Mike closed his eyes to more fully enjoy the sensations. He hadn't expected this. He thought they would fuck hard and fast—and he was okay with that—but what he got instead was a tender lover, a man whose lips brushed him soft as butterflies even as their cocks moved together, hard and slick.

When he reached Mike's lower arm, Goran paused. "It's healing well," he said.

That was true. Mike had abandoned the wound dressings several days earlier, and new skin had grown over the cut already, pink and healthy.

"You'll have a scar," Goran said.

"I don't care."

"And you really don't mind about mine?"

Christ. Mike never would have guessed a man as beautiful and strong as Goran could be so insecure. With considerable effort, he rolled them over. He took a moment to admire Goran sprawled beneath him, hair fanned on the soft green moss, lips wet and suckable. And then Mike proceeded to kiss every one of Goran's scars. It took him a long time—there were a lot of them—and sometimes he had to tug Goran's pliant body this way and that. But when he was finished, Goran gazed up at him with eyes gone soft and wondering.

Mike couldn't quite bear to look back. He closed his eyes and rubbed his cheek against the hair on Goran's chest. Goran purred beneath him like a great cat, in sharp contrast to Mike's original comparison of him as a Newfoundland dog. Mike was used to his partners being taller than him, bigger and hairier, but he'd never had one quite as monumental as Goran. It was a little overwhelming, in a totally wonderful way. Even better when Goran stroked Mike's lower back and then massaged his ass.

"Can I fuck you, Mike? Please?"

Mike's immediate instinct was to answer *Hell yes!*, but he stopped to think about practical matters. There was the safer-sex issue, for one. Mike had always been very careful about that—he insisted on condoms and was tested regularly. He was fairly certain he wasn't harboring any nasty pathogens. But he didn't know about Goran. Maybe there was no HIV in this world, but there might very well be other unhappy surprises, and with no antibiotics in sight. Well, he decided, STDs were not the biggest threat he was facing right now. He'd take his chances.

But that raised a second issue, which was lube. Or more accurately, the lack thereof. He'd used a few odd things when he wanted to beat off and nothing else was available—hair conditioner, aloe vera gel, hand lotion, and once a handful of margarine. But he'd never tried any of those things for internal use, and in any case, he didn't exactly have a tub of I Can't Believe It's Not Butter! lying around.

Goran misunderstood his hesitation. "You can fuck me instead if you want, Mike. I'd enjoy that. Or we could—"

"No, I like your original plan just fine. Just thinking about how we're going to do it."

With a grin, Goran rolled them over again. "Less thinking, more doing, pretty boy." He gently flipped Mike onto his stomach and spread Mike's legs. For a heart-stopping moment, Mike was afraid Goran was going to dive in just like that. But he shouldn't have worried—what Goran actually did was part Mike's asscheeks and start licking at his hole.

"Ohh," Mike said—a gasp more than a word. He tucked his knees underneath himself to give Goran better access. Goran rewarded him by inserting his hot, slick tongue.

"Oh God." Mike wasn't even sure which god he was invoking— maybe this kind of thing fell within Agata's territory. Maybe he was invoking all of them, because Goran inside him felt so fucking good. Um, a little too good, actually. "Gonna— Fuck me, Gor," he choked out between gritted teeth.

Luckily, Goran was quick to obey. He removed his tongue, gave Mike's ass a quick and friendly squeeze, and repositioned himself. And then he slowly pushed his cock inside.

It hurt. Although Mike's muscles had been loosened and he was more than ready psychologically, spit and precome didn't make for the easiest going, and it had been a long time since any man had gone where Goran was going now. But Goran showed remarkable self-control, easing in very slowly, and Mike moved rapidly past the point where he cared about the pain. "More!" he ordered. "Move!" Yes, perhaps he'd been called a pushy bottom on more than one occasion.

Goran, attentive and compliant, gave him more. He thrust a few times, very slowly, and when Mike groaned happily back at him, he sped up. But after only a few moments of that, he squiggled an arm under Mike's chest and, without breaking the contact between their lower halves, drew Mike upright. This left Goran in a deep squat, one hand behind himself for balance and one wrapped very nicely around Mike's cock. Mike, in the meantime, remained impaled on Goran's cock, straddling his lap, and had only to flex his thighs in order to drag himself up and down, to feel the good burn in his ass and the sweet friction around his dick. A strong, athletic lover was a wonderful thing.

Now that he was in the driver's seat, Mike could move things along more quickly. He tilted his head back and closed his eyes. Every time he rose or fell, sparks of pure pleasure danced through his body. He dimly realized that he could be as loud as he wanted—no neighbors to complain about the noise around here—and with that realization he released something tight within himself, a door he'd been keeping carefully locked for years. His movements became quicker and less rhythmic, Goran's almost wordless chanting rang in his ears—"Yes, yes, yes, please please please!"—and with a roar that echoed through the trees, Mike came.

Goran shouted and his arm gave way. They collapsed in a sweaty pile of flesh, their hearts beating madly.

But Goran was still capable of surprising Mike, because even before they'd caught their breaths, he scooped Mike into a tight embrace and murmured softly against his neck: "Thank you. Thank you so much, Mike."

Chapter 9

THEY NAPPED awhile with limbs entwined and then went for another swim, as much for the fun of it as to wash up. By the time they got out of the pool, the afternoon had turned to early evening and their clothing was dry. Goran put on his garments and disappeared into the woods. He returned shortly with another marblebird.

They didn't speak much that evening, but the fire wasn't the only thing glowing. Mike felt a warm sense of contentment deep inside. It was more than the aftermath of really spectacular sex. They touched often: a hand on an arm, one leg pressing against another. There was a certain depth to Goran's smile that hadn't existed before.

They made love again before they went to sleep, and if anything it was even better than the first time. They settled down near the dying fire, no longer keeping a few feet of neutral territory between their bodies. But as comfortable as Mike was, snuggled back against Goran's warm bulk, sleep didn't come easily. He was worried about the depth of his contentment, the strength of his feelings for Goran. The fact that his goal was to leave this world and return home.

"Stupid," he whispered, too quietly to awaken Goran. "This can't last." Wouldn't last. He'd just have to enjoy it while he could.

MIKE AND Goran arrived in Varesh well fed by the game Goran caught, and very well fucked. They'd tried out a variety of positions as they traveled, which meant that the journey had taken longer than it should have. Neither of them considered the time ill spent, however.

Varesh was a large city. Its buildings spilled well beyond the original city walls, and the traffic—people and draft animals and carts—was heavy. Located on a broad plain at the confluence of four rivers, Varesh had boat traffic as well. Many small canals laced the central part of the city, inside the walls. "It's like Venice without the sea," Mike observed shortly after they arrived. "And without the Italian food." He would have killed for pizza.

Goran had become used to Mike making references he didn't understand. Now he simply shrugged. "We can get food here. Maybe."

They moved through the crowds toward the center of the city. Goran made a good leader here, using his bulk to advantage as he pushed his way through. Mike mostly followed in his wake, trying not to lose him or to gape like a hick tourist.

But it was hard not to gape. Varesh was clearly more prosperous than anyplace Mike had visited in this world. The shops and market stalls burst with goods for sale, the outsides of the houses were decorated with statues and paintings and various other gewgaws, and many of the people wore richly ornamented clothes and shiny jewelry. Intersections and public squares were dotted with statues of men and women and weird half-human creatures. Instead of wells there were fountains adorned with spouting fish, scrollwork, and other frippery.

Goran had warned him to be careful of thieves in Varesh. Mike didn't have much for anyone to steal, but he kept a careful eye on people around him and wished for one of those neck wallet things that were supposed to keep pickpockets away from your passport and credit cards. After the peace and solitude of the forest, the crush here was a little overwhelming. Mike was relieved when they sat on the stone stairs outside a temple in a relatively quiet square.

"Is this the shrine?" asked Mike.

"No. You just looked like you needed a break."

"Thanks." Mike slumped comfortably and watched a gaggle of screaming children chase a leather ball, kicking and throwing it to one another. If there were rules to whatever game they were playing, he couldn't fathom them. "You know, it didn't occur to me when we were in the forest, but how come there's a pretty nice road through the middle of it but there was nobody else on it?"

"It's the wrong time of year. Earlier in the spring, hundreds of people from Varesh would have passed through on their way to their family farms near Tesli, in the foothills of the Forgotten Mountains. They'll raise hops and glowberries and barley there. And at the end of autumn, when the last harvests are done, they'll return here."

"That seems like a lot of… movement."

"That's how it's always been done. Nobody wants to live in Tesli during the winter. It's bitterly cold. Besides, they can make a better living by coming back to Varesh and brewing ale and wine."

Mike figured he shouldn't criticize. He knew people who spent hours daily in commutes from the Central Valley to the San Francisco Bay Area.

One of the kids threw the ball wildly. It bounced off the pavement and almost into Goran's lap. He caught it neatly and tossed it back, earning him cheers from the rowdy gang.

"Nice arm," Mike said. He'd played Little League and made the high school varsity team but wasn't good enough to pull down an athletic scholarship in college. But even when they'd grown up, he and Marie would go over to their parents' house to watch games with their father. A transplant from the Midwest, Dad refused to transfer his loyalties and remained a White Sox fan his entire life. He'd taken special glee in rooting against Oakland. Benny liked the A's. Maybe that explained part of his parents' antipathy for the guy.

As Goran watched the children, Mike remembered his story. On his own at ten years old. Did he and Pavo ever have time to play ball, or were they too busy trying to survive? Christ, at ten Mike still insisted on sleeping with a night-light and considered himself very accomplished when he managed to toast a Pop-Tart all by himself.

"What are you supposed to offer at this shrine?" Goran asked.

"Not a clue. This time my helpful author guy didn't bother to say. Man, I hope he didn't quit his day job, because he makes a shitty travel guide. But hey, he did inform me that goats give more milk and hens lay bigger eggs if you sing to them every evening at bedtime. So there's that."

One of the kids was a runty girl with badly cut red hair. When the ball rolled to a stop at her feet, she picked it up and then stubbornly refused to let it go. Some of the bigger kids began to yell at her, at which point she burst into tears. Then another girl—a larger, older version of the ball hog—punched one of the bullies, and a miniature brawl erupted. The fight was amusing, but Goran stood. "Let's go before it gets too late. The shrine is still a good distance from here."

He wasn't lying. They walked for another hour, this time mostly through less fancy neighborhoods. Once they came to a square where a crowd of adults was yelling and calling out insults. At the center was a tall, thick stone post on a little pedestal. A man was chained to the post, his bound wrists tethered high over his head. He was shirtless and his pants were hardly more than rags; his back was a mass of bleeding welts. He moved around as much as his chains permitted, trying to avoid the garbage and small stones the crowd pitched at him, but he kept getting hit anyway.

"Goran," Mike began, coming to a halt.

Goran grabbed his arm and dragged him out of the square. "We can't help him."

"But—"

"He's a criminal. If you try to interfere, you'll end up just like him."

"Will… will they kill him?"

"I don't know. Depends what he did and depends on the mood of the crowd." They were in a narrow alley now. It smelled like cat piss. Goran let go of Mike's arm and turned to look at him. "Don't they use the pillar in California?"

"No."

"But you do have criminals?"

"Oh, we have plenty. Mostly we put them in prison."

A large puddle of unidentifiable but disgusting goo took up most of the alley; Mike and Goran had to hug the wall to avoid stepping in it. "What's a prison?" Goran asked. "Is it like a noose?"

"It's a building. A not very nice building. They lock up the bad guys for… a bunch of years, usually. Depends what they did."

Goran looked appalled. "They lock them up and don't let them out?"

"Yes."

"I'd rather have the pillar. Or the noose."

Mike nodded. Goran was so at home in the forest. Mike couldn't picture him encased in concrete and iron. He'd be like a tiger in one of those old-fashioned zoos, the ones with the tiny cages that drove the animals to pace and, ultimately, to insanity.

They emerged from the alley into a neat, quiet street lined with what appeared to be closed-up shops. No other people were in the street, just a cat napping in a patch of sunshine. Goran stopped in the middle and looked around in confusion. "This isn't right."

"Are we lost?"

"No, it's not that. These shops should all be open. They sell little statues and parchment-paper money to give as offerings at the Temple of Four Winds." He gestured toward the end of the street, where a large building of white stone squatted.

"Is that a problem?" Mike asked.

"Your shrine is in the temple. There's a room in the center where they used to make human sacrifices a very long time ago. That's where Alina's shrine is."

Two young men came from a side street near the temple, heading toward Mike and Goran. They walked slowly, arm in arm, laughing over some shared joke. They didn't even glance away from each other until Goran stepped into their path, at which point they looked slightly alarmed. "We don't have anything to steal," said the shorter one.

"And there are guards just around the corner if you try," his companion added. He was a little chubby.

Goran raised his hands placatingly. "We're not thieves. My master is on a pilgrimage."

The men visibly relaxed, and the taller man spoke. "That's too bad, because the temple is closed."

"Closed?" Mike and Goran said in unison.

"Until the next full moon. Until then, the priests are in seclusion. They do this every year. Didn't you know?"

Mike muttered curses against the guidebook author under his breath, and Goran looked distressed. "That's three weeks from now," Goran said.

"Sorry. Nobody can disturb the priests. Two hundred years ago there was a huge fire. Half the city burned. People pounded on the temple doors, begging the priests to come out, but the doors stayed locked. And when the fire burned out and everyone returned, not a building was standing in this entire quarter except for the temple. The gods spared the priests because they were so pious."

Well, that was just dandy. Goran rubbed his forehead. "I suppose there's no place for pilgrims to stay, then?"

The men shook their heads. "Not until the temple reopens," the shorter one said. Then the men continued their walk, heads leaning close together.

"I am so sorry, Mike. I'm your guide, and I should have known. If we'd traveled faster—"

"Don't." Mike put a hand on Goran's shoulder. "I enjoyed our… detour. A lot. It was better than the best vacation I ever had. We'll just have to wait three weeks." He hoped Alina was patient. His family back home no doubt already assumed he was dead. He was sorry for their added grief, but since he wasn't at all sure he was ever going to return home, a few more weeks didn't much matter.

Goran still looked upset but also relieved that Mike was taking the news so well. "We can return to the forest if you want. If we stay here, we'll have to find a place to sleep and some way to get food."

As much as Mike had enjoyed his time with Goran, he was really missing a bed, even if it was a crappy one. Besides, he'd run out of tooth-cleaning twigs and his soap was down to a thin sliver. "Do you think there's any chance we can stay?" he asked.

After several minutes of silent thought, Goran nodded. "I think so. If you don't mind a little bit of… burglary."

Mike thought of that poor guy at the pillar and swallowed hard. "Okeydoke."

They left the temple neighborhood at a brisk pace and twisted and turned down a number of streets. Sometimes they crossed small stone bridges just like the ones in Venice. Eventually they came to a district that straddled one of the rivers and nudged up against one of the city walls. The houses here were freestanding and square, each two stories high and made of timber and stone. Each house had a large yard in back, with small outbuildings and stacks of barrels. The air in this part of town smelled like fermenting fruit.

"The people from Tesli live here," Goran explained. "There shouldn't be many people around until late autumn."

"So… we're going to do some housesitting?"

"I think we could stay in one of the sheds and nobody would notice. I'm not so sure about the houses themselves. They might have someone staying there."

There went Mike's dreams of actual beds. But a shed floor was probably not too lumpy, and the roof would protect them from rain. "Sounds like a plan."

"Good. Wait here."

Mike sat on the low wall along the river's edge, dangling his feet and watching the water move sluggishly by. The river was very dirty, full of debris and smelling even more strongly than the fermenting fruit. When it reached the city wall, it disappeared through a dark tunnel too low to allow boat traffic. A sewage system of sorts, he guessed. Not environmentally friendly, but effective.

Goran returned soon, smiling. "I found us a place."

Mike rose from the wall and followed him. The house Goran chose wasn't on the wide street that paralleled the river but rather on a narrow side street. That was good. Less traffic. The house looked neglected, with a second-story shutter hanging by a single hinge and weeds poking through the paving stones near the front door. The house hid the shed from the street, and behind the shed rose a tall stone wall. The yard was littered with broken bits of wood and pottery.

"Look," Goran said, pushing open the shed door. Mike peeked inside. It was mostly empty, apart from a thick layer of dust. There were a few stoneware jugs, a rough wooden table, some empty shelves. An iron bed had been set against one wall, mattress and all.

Goran bounced inside and patted the bed, sending a cloud of dust into the air. "It's almost a palace!"

"Almost."

"I think this family is gone for good. Nobody's lived here for a long while. The neighbors might notice if we moved into the house, but nobody will see us here if we're careful."

"Why is there a bed?"

"This family made wine. See the bottles?" He pointed at a tall shelf where, sure enough, a couple of empty glass bottles lay on their sides. "When the new wine is bottled, it needs to be turned every six hours to prevent settling. I suppose it was easiest for the winemaker to sleep in here instead of walking back and forth all night."

"Well, hooray for lazy winemakers."

Still happy with himself, Goran bounded over to Mike, wrapped him in strong arms, and pulled him close. "Do you think we can both fit on that mattress?" he purred into Mike's ear.

"I'm sure as hell willing to give it a try." Mike's words were muffled by Goran's chest, but Goran probably understood them anyway.

SOMEHOW MAKING the shed habitable became Mike's job, while Goran hit the pavement in search of food and supplies. "I never wanted to be a housewife," Mike grumbled as he drew water from the pump in the yard into a bucket. "My mother was never a housewife. Even my grandmas worked." He dipped a bottle into the bucket and watched it fill. The water looked clean enough. He had to hope it didn't come from the nearby river.

Once he'd filled all the bottles and set them on the table, he snuck into the house in search of cleaning supplies. The house wasn't much better furnished than the shed, but he did discover a broom with a broken handle and some lace curtains that he could use as dust cloths. Then he swept and scrubbed and dusted until the sun set. After that, there wasn't much for him to do but sit in the darkness, listening to his stomach grumble and waiting for Goran. He tried some of the water. It tasted okay and didn't kill him right away.

Goran looked tired when he returned, although he grinned when he lit a candle and saw the condition of the room. "You cleaned!"

"And you found a candle."

"More than that." He shoved the base of the candle into a jug, creating a candleholder any Italian restaurant would be proud of. He set the jug on the newly cleaned table, then upended onto the table a fabric sack he'd been carrying. Food tumbled out: bread, cheese, sausage, apples. Enough to tide them over for a few meals at least.

"How'd you score all that?" Mike asked. He pictured Goran skulking through a market, stealthily stuffing food into his sack. Except Goran was a little too big to skulk successfully.

"I got a job."

Mike blinked. "A job?"

"As a stevedore, loading and unloading boats. Nobody's supposed to hire me because I don't belong to the guild, but because I'm so strong I talked someone into it. He's paying me less than the other men, and he'll probably expect me to work twice as hard, but I don't mind. It will keep us fed for a few weeks."

"That's great, Gor. But how'd you get the cash for this haul?" As soon as the question was out of his mouth, however, Mike saw the answer: Goran's scabbard was empty. "Oh no, Gor, not your sword!"

Goran shrugged. "He's holding it for me. I asked him to loan me a few coins so we could eat tonight and tomorrow. This way he knows I'll come back. He'll return it to me in a few days."

Mike felt very uncomfortable about Goran pawning his sword. Along with his knife, it was the only valuable thing he owned. He slept with it on, for gods' sake. And the reason it wasn't hanging from his hip right now was because of Mike. He was why they were stuck in Varesh for three weeks, waiting to apologize to a god and squatting in an empty shed instead of sleeping in the forest.

"I'm sorry, Goran," he said.

"It's *fine*. Let's eat, all right? I'm famished. The bread was still warm when I bought it!"

They sat on the newly cleaned slate floor and ate. The meal was delicious—fresh bread, tangy cheese with a hint of herbs, spicy sausage. Goran had bought a jug of ale too. "Wow," said Mike, impressed after his first swallow. "This is decent stuff."

"Probably brewed very close by. Varesh is known for its ale and wine."

"Hey, Gor? Do you think your new boss would give me a job too? If we double our income—"

"No." Goran patted Mike's knee. "I told you, he only hired me because I'm so strong."

"I'm not weak!"

Goran sighed. "I know. But look at us. I'm big. I can lift heavy things, and I can kill things. It's what I'm good for. You, though— you're smart and you know things and you figure things out. Pavo was like that. He was a little on the small side, like you. But he planned everything. If we had a problem, he solved it. I always wished I could do that."

"Goran, I haven't solved a damn thing since I got here. You've done everything."

"That's only because you're new to this place." Goran drank a few mouthfuls of ale. "Back home, back in… California… you do solve problems, don't you?"

"I guess." It was Mike's turn to sigh. "I'm a fiscal analyst."

"I don't know what that means."

"It means I help a company handle its money better. I tell it how much money it has and where it's coming from, what it's being spent on. I help them make better decisions what to do with it." Well, didn't that sound exciting.

But Goran smiled. "See? I knew it. Look, I'll earn enough. You can rest. Explore the city a little or read your book." His grin turned wicked. "You can spend all day planning how we'll please each other that night."

"I think we've been doing pretty well without planning anything," Mike said.

"Let's finish our meal and see what we haven't planned today."

They didn't go to bed right after dinner, though. Mike first persuaded Goran to help him carry the mattress out into the yard and then to hold it upright while Mike beat it with a stick. Not only did he want to get the dust off it, but he wasn't sure what small creatures might have made a home there. His standards for sleeping arrangements had sunk considerably over the past weeks, but he still wasn't crazy about sharing a bed with anything but Goran. He tried to keep the mattress beating relatively quiet in case the neighbors might hear.

When the mattress was back on the bed and they'd used the well to wash up, they stripped each other. Goran liked to play with the waistband of Mike's briefs—elastic was a technological wonder to him. Mike just liked the excuse to move his hands over Goran's big, firm frame and watch tantalizing skin appear bit by bit.

As Goran's trousers dropped to the floor, a small cloth purse fell too. Goran bent to retrieve it, then dangled it in front of Mike. His lecherous grin had returned. "I bought something else too."

"Oh?"

Goran opened the purse and pulled out a tiny glass vial. "See?"

"I'm guessing that's not poppers."

"Huh?" Goran gave his usual Mike's-spouting-gibberish shrug. "Oil. Slippery, slick oil."

"Ah!" They'd been making do just fine, but Mike couldn't say he wasn't thankful. He squished a handful of Goran's ass. "You're as good at gathering as you are at hunting."

The bed would have been a very tight fit for Goran alone; the two of them together could barely climb on without one of them falling off. But Mike wasn't about to give up his precious mattress. After a bit of wrangling and twisting, they found something that worked: Goran lay flat on his back—feet hanging off the end of the bed—while Mike straddled him on his knees. Then Goran carefully, diligently worked the oil into Mike until they were both gasping with need, and Mike sank down onto Goran's well-lubed cock.

He liked this position, even if it involved a lot of work on his part. It meant he could set the pace and angle himself for best results, and it meant Goran was free to play with Mike's cock and nipples. But best of all, it meant he had a good view of the beautiful man beneath him, of Goran's hair escaping its leather tie to fan out widely, of Goran's warm green eyes. Even better when they were fucking by candlelight, because the small glow made the two of them an island and made the rest of the world—the rest of all worlds—disappear.

"Please," Goran groaned when Mike wickedly paused with only the head of Goran's cock breaching him. Goran tried to buck up with his hips. Mike loved to watch him writhe. "Please, please, Mike. Gods!"

Mike took pity on him, lowering himself exquisitely slowly. He realized he was biting his lip—he tasted blood—but that didn't matter at the moment. Not when he was so wonderfully filled, and not when calloused hands were stroking Mike's needy cock and caressing his balls. And when Goran arched his neck and climaxed with a growl, Mike forgot everything except how good the two of them felt together. His climax hit him like an electric jolt, and his come spurted across Goran's chest and face. Mike used a finger to scrape a little of the pearly fluid from Goran's chest hair, then slowly licked his finger clean. Goran groaned like a dying man.

Mike collapsed onto Goran's torso. He felt like he'd just run a marathon, only messier. Goran nuzzled at his neck and gently stroked his lower back. "Am I good, Mike?" he whispered.

"What?"

"At fucking. Do I make you happy?"

"Jesus, Gor. My brains are pretty much liquefied now, so I'd say yes. You're amazing."

Goran gave a small, satisfied grunt. "Good. I want to make you happy, Mike."

"I… thank you." Mike didn't know how else to respond. But maybe that was enough, because Goran kissed his temple and gave him a small squeeze.

They got out of bed and gave each other a quick wipe with water from one of the bottles. "I'd love a bath," Mike said a little wistfully. "And clean clothes."

"There are bathhouses here. Once I earn a few extra coppers, we can go."

"With warm water, even?"

Goran laughed. "All the warm water you could want."

"Sounds like heaven."

They remained naked because the night was warm. After blowing the candle out, they found a position on the bed that was reasonably comfortable. Goran curled up on his side, his back against the wall, and Mike smooshed back against him with his ass nestled nicely against

Goran's soft cock. Goran's right arm was underneath Mike, who worried it might fall asleep but decided not to say anything. This was too pleasant. He'd never been much of a cuddler before, had rarely even spent the night with another man. Even when he and Benny dated, each would usually sleep at his own apartment. So this was nice, and he felt safe.

He was very nearly asleep when Goran kissed the back of his neck. "Mike?"

"Hmm?"

"Do they have stevedores in California?"

"Some. Not many. We have machines that do most of the heavy lifting."

"Oh." There was a short pause. "What about guards? You work with all that money. You must have someone to guard it, right?"

Oh, fuck. Mike swallowed hard. He decided that bank accounts and the like were too much to explain. "Yeah, Gor. We have guards."

Goran paused again, and Mike hoped he'd fallen asleep. No such luck. "Mike? When you go back to California… maybe I could come with?"

"Goran—"

"I know I don't know my way around there like I do Nenahde, but I can learn. I can hunt for you and guard you. You wouldn't need to give me the book, and you know I don't need much. Just you."

With his cold heart aching, Mike turned around in Goran's embrace. "Why would you want to do that, Gor? This is your home."

"I have no home!" Goran lowered his voice. "I haven't had a home since Pavo—since I left Strazha. But I think… I think I could be home with *you*, Mike. Wherever you are."

Mike was glad for the darkness. "I can't, Goran. I… I'm sorry. I can't take you to California."

"Oh. All right," replied Goran, sounding for all the world like a lost, disappointed child. "Good night."

Mike rolled back into his original position. Soon Goran was snoring in his ear, but Mike lay awake for a very long time.

Chapter 10

THERE WERE indeed bathhouses in Varesh. Mike and Goran used them twice weekly, and they were wonderful oases of hot water, steam, good soap, and clean towels. A barber worked at the bathhouse. He used a straight razor instead of a knife, but Mike had to admit the results were no better than Goran's had been. Goran bought Mike an extra set of clothes. Like the ones Agata stole for him, this tunic and trousers were also used, but they were of better quality and in better condition. The tunic had a pewter button to hold the deep V-neck closed and some simple embroidery at the shoulders and hem. Even better, Goran found him boots, heavy boots of brown leather with weird toggles instead of laces. Mike enjoyed clomping around the cobblestones in them. He didn't discard the sandals yet, although the soles were badly worn.

Squeaky-clean, freshly shaved, and in Mike's case attired in new clothes, they decided to have dinner someplace a little nicer than the divey taverns where they'd been eating for the previous two weeks. As they walked down the cobbled streets together, Mike felt absurdly like he was going on a date. "It's a nice evening," he said.

"It was hot this afternoon. We had to load barrels of ale onto three ships in a row. By the time we were finished, I was ready to dive into one of those barrels myself."

Mike nodded. Goran had resumed drinking heavily in the evenings, and his cheer had assumed that air of falseness he'd lost in the forest. But he hadn't mentioned California again, for which Mike was grateful. "I was hot too, and I wasn't doing anything but sitting around."

"You swept the floor and filled all our bottles with water."

"Big deal."

"It's nice to have someone taking care of things while I'm at work," said Goran quietly.

Mike didn't answer, and in any case, a moment later they were seating themselves at a table at the edge of a wide street. For several blocks, the street was lined with tables and chairs. The air smelled of good food, people chatted happily while they ate and drank, and innkeepers and their helpers scurried around. Well-dressed people promenaded slowly up and down the street in pairs and small groups. Sometimes a few of them would stop and talk to others, creating a temporary pedestrian traffic jam. Apparently this was the place to see and be seen on an early-summer evening.

As soon as Mike and Goran sat down, a half-grown boy brought them goblets of red wine and small cups filled with a liquor that made Mike cough. Goran laughed. "It's good for you. It has honey and herbs."

"I feel like my throat is on fire."

"Good! That means it's healthy."

It didn't taste bad, actually, just very strong. Mike finished his off, although not all in one swallow like Goran. Once his taste buds recovered, he tried the wine. It was very nice.

The restaurant had no menus, which made sense if few people could read. Apparently you got whatever was fresh that day. Tonight that was a tasty, oily fish served whole, head and all. It looked surprised to be on Mike's plate. On the side were greens cooked with potatoes and garlic and more herbs, lots of warm crusty bread, and some kind of savory pudding. It was all delicious.

They drank more wine with dinner, and after the boy cleared away the plates, he brought them a fresh bottle. This variety was white and sweet.

Goran moved his chair around so he sat next to Mike, both of them facing the street. "Did you like it?" Goran asked.

"Definitely." In truth, as good as the food had been, Mike had actually preferred the half-raw, half-burned game he'd shared with Goran in the forest. But he didn't say so. "I feel like I'm living it up more than a pilgrim ought to."

"Aw, not really. I've seen wealthy pilgrims. They have their servants following along a half league behind them with all their things. That way they can say they traveled with very little."

It was strangely comforting to learn that even in this world, the rich found technicalities and loopholes the poor couldn't afford. "Well, I'm glad you're not walking a half league behind me."

Goran grinned.

Mike poured himself another cup of wine and topped off Goran's while he was at it. He felt just a bit buzzed. He felt good. His thoughts were unfocused as he gazed out at the passing crowds without really seeing them.

"Meliach?"

Mike startled to awareness as Goran leapt to his feet, hand on the hilt of his sword. He didn't draw it, which was probably just as well; the two wealthy men standing in front of their table were each flanked by an armed guard of their own.

"Meliach?" repeated one of the men. He was handsome, maybe thirty-five, with blond hair and a neatly trimmed beard. "Whatever are you doing *here*? And wearing *that*?"

Mike blinked at him. "Sorry. Don't know what you're talking about. You must have me confused—"

"Don't be ridiculous! As if I wouldn't know you." He glared pointedly at Goran. "Would you please tell your brute to stand down?"

Mike tapped Goran's arm. "It's okay, Gor. Have a seat."

Reluctantly, Goran sat down. But he kept his hand on his sword, and his body remained tense. The other guards visibly relaxed, while the other rich man—a balding guy in his fifties—watched avidly. He seemed to be enjoying the entertainment.

"Thank you," Blondie said. "You're going quite a bit... rougher than usual, Mel. What's going on?"

"Look. I'm not whoever you think I am, okay?"

"Come now! We've spent far too much time together for me to be mistaken." The expression on Blondie's face clearly conveyed what sort of time that had been. Dammit, why did Mike have to run into one of the lord's fuck buddies?

"I don't know you," Mike said firmly. "And my name is Mike Carlson. Not Meliach."

"He's on a pilgrimage to Alina's shrines," Goran inserted. Mike wished he hadn't but tried not to show it.

Blondie's pale eyebrows rose. "A pilgrimage? That's rich, Mel! It's not like you to play games like this. I'll look forward to hearing the entire tale when next we meet. For now, though, I'll leave you to your… piety." Laughing loudly, Blondie and his companions walked away.

"Who was that, Mike?"

"Dunno. Never seem him before in my life." Which was true enough.

Goran gave him a long, serious look. "He seemed to know you."

"No, he seemed to know someone named Meliach. I'm not him."

After a pause, Goran nodded. "All right. But it's only— You have secrets, don't you?"

"So do you," Mike snapped.

"Not secrets. Just… things I don't like to talk about."

And then Mike felt guilty and miserable. "Sorry. Let's head back, okay?"

"I'm sorry too. I shouldn't pry. I'm only your guide."

"Dammit, Gor, you're a hell of a lot more than that, and you know it." Fuck. "C'mon, big guy. Let's go." He stood and squeezed Goran's shoulder.

Goran slowly rose. Neither said another word as they walked back to their shed. They had sex that night, as they did almost every night, and it was as sweet and tender and hot as always. And Mike's cold heart shattered.

Chapter 11

THE STREET leading to the Temple of Four Winds was transformed. Before it had been tidy and peaceful. Now it was a bustling, rowdy place. Every shop was open, and every shop owner loudly touted his or her wares. *Finest icons in the south! Prayer scrolls custom-made! Top-quality parchment money here!*

Crowds of shoppers jostled one another, haggling over religious trinkets, munching on skewers of roasted meat from vending carts, catching up on gossip. Goran had already explained that few of these people were pilgrims. The vast majority were locals who were eager to catch up on a month's worth of favors asked and thanks owed to the gods. The atmosphere reminded Mike of the county fair his family used to attend when he was a kid. No puke-inducing rides, but there was a good variety of street entertainers. The most popular were men and women in gaudy, exaggerated costumes who pretended to engage in various sinful acts and then suffer the wrath of one god or another. There were beggars as well. Goran tossed leekas to several of them, telling Mike it would bring good luck.

A line stretched in front of the temple, with burly men and women in bright-red tunics trying to keep everyone orderly. "Bouncers?" Mike asked, pointing at two of them.

"Priests."

"It's like a really hip club that I'm not going to be cool enough to get into."

Goran gave him his patient look. "They'll let us in. We just have to wait."

And they did. The line snaked all the way down the temple stairs and onto the street, but it did move. Slowly. "It's like Disneyland," Mike muttered, earning him a bewildered look. Some of the street performers concentrated their efforts near the line. They warbled tunes, performed gymnastic feats, and told jokes Mike couldn't comprehend. A few of them just stood and preached. Mike didn't understand them, but he got the impression there were a whole lot of gods. He wondered if keeping track of them was like keeping track of a baseball team. Did they have trading cards?

At very long last, Mike and Goran made it to the front of the line. The bouncer-priest who stood there was even bigger than Goran, and he didn't look nearly as rested as a guy ought to after a month of retreat. "Whom do you entreat today?" he boomed.

"Um, Alina," answered Mike. The people in line behind him murmured. Mike had the impression that Alina wasn't the most popular god around here.

The priest didn't look especially approving either. But he nodded regally and clapped his hands. Another priest came running up—a cute young girl with frizzy brown curls. "Alina," said the behemoth.

The girl frowned but nodded. Then she turned to Mike. "This way, please." She took off at a healthy clip.

Mike didn't get a chance to look carefully at the interior of the temple. He noticed it was big and mazelike, with voices, sobs, and chants echoing weirdly off the stone floors and walls. The place smelled odd too—a confusing mixture of incense, food, sweat, and perfume. Statues, scrolls, paintings, and altars lurked everywhere. No wonder those poor priests needed an annual vacation.

Mike's small party came to a door of dark wood and iron. It looked heavy and forbidding, like something from a dungeon. Their priest came to a halt. "Alina's shrine," she announced. Of course. The door had a weird hook thing instead of a knob; she wiggled it a bit and then pushed the door open. "I will wait here. Knock when you are ready to leave."

Were they going to be locked in? Great. Mike started to step inside but stopped. "Excuse me. Can you tell me what kind of offering

I'm supposed to make?" He hadn't thought to bring anything, and he was going to be pissed at himself if he had to go out to buy something, then stand in line again. He also hoped it wasn't another call for blood.

She scowled. "Tears."

"Tears. Like… crying?"

"Yes."

Fuck.

Mike entered with Goran close at his heels. The door closed behind them with a boom.

It was a fucking scary shrine. There were no windows since it was at the center of the building. There was plenty of light, however—cast by dozens and dozens of enormous candles impaled on iron stands. Between the candleholders were bones. Human bones, stacked neatly, with skulls over here and femurs over there. Most had been painted dark red with what he really hoped was not blood. Smack-dab in the center of the room, a large glass bowl balanced atop a low pedestal decorated with scenes of death and mayhem. "This Alina chick is kinda goth," Mike muttered. "If she lived in California, I bet she'd listen to Marilyn Manson and wear a shitload of black."

"Mike?" Goran looked seriously spooked.

"Sorry. I should be more respectful, I guess." He sighed heavily. "I don't know how to give her tears, Gor."

"You cry."

"Yeah, I got that. But I *don't* cry. The last time I did, I was twelve years old and I'd just busted my arm."

"But… you've had sad things happen to you."

Mike twitched a shoulder. "Sure. But I just… I deal. I'm not emotional. Never have been." Coldhearted.

Goran crossed his arms over his chest. "I don't believe you."

"You've been spending a lot of time with me. Do I strike you as a guy who loses his cool easily?"

"No…."

"Well." Mike kicked out his foot irritably, almost knocking over a pile of rib bones. "So I'm screwed."

"I can cry."

Mike looked up at Goran. He had a clear mental image of his lover collapsed on his knees, hands covering his face, great sobs wracking his body. Crying over his lost mother, his murdered father, his destroyed home. And then there was the mysterious Pavo. Every time Goran spoke of him, his eyes filled with pain.

"No," Mike said. "I think they have to be my tears. It would be cheating if I used someone else's. Damn. It'd be a lot easier just to cut myself again."

"You fear emotional pain more than physical."

"I don't…. It's not that I fear it, Goran. I don't *feel* it. At least, not like other people do."

Goran's arms remained crossed. "I don't believe that. Things have made you sad."

"Yeah, sure, but—"

"So think about one of those things."

Crap. Mike sat down and crossed his legs. The floor was marble, slick and cold. Goran sat opposite him, looking at him expectantly.

"My father died," Mike said. "Not… not like yours. I mean, I was grown already and nobody murdered him. He'd been feeling kind of sick for a while, but not sick enough to see a doctor over it. Just heartburn mostly, and he felt tired all the time, and he was losing weight. By the time he felt miserable enough to do something about it, things were too far along. Stomach cancer, but it had metastasized."

Goran was listening intently, although much of what Mike was saying must have been unintelligible to him. "Was he sick for a long time?"

"Over a year. They tried surgery and chemo and radiation, but God, all that shit was so hard on him too. And none of it worked. He just got sicker.

"Mom was working full-time and spending all the rest of her time taking care of him, driving him to the doctor, sitting in the hospital with him. I was afraid she was going to get sick too. Marie and I helped out as much as we could, but we were both starting our careers. Mom and Dad wanted us to concentrate on that."

"They loved you," Goran said.

Mike smiled slightly. "Yeah." He closed his eyes and pictured his father near the very end, lying gray and shrunken in a hospice bed. Dad had been so weak then, groggy from the heavy doses of pain meds. But he still liked to hear his children talk about what they'd been doing that day. Mike would give him summaries of the latest White Sox game. On days when there hadn't been a game, Mike would make one up. *Lee and Ordóñez played really well today*, he'd say. *Konerko kind of sucked, though.*

"Mike?" Goran's hand was on Mike's knee.

"He died in the middle of the night. Mom was asleep by his side. It was quiet, no fuss. Dad was like that. By then everyone was thankful it was over, really."

"Did you cry?"

"No. Don't get me wrong—I loved Dad, and I was really sad to lose him. But I stayed strong for Mom and Marie, you know?"

Even now, he wasn't choked up about it. His father had died far too young, but people did. Dad had a good life until he got sick. He was a happy man, and when he left the world, he was all right with himself and everyone else.

Mike sighed. "This isn't working. That's pretty much the worst thing that's ever happened to me, and I can't cry over it."

Goran scratched his jaw thoughtfully. "Maybe something more recent. You had to leave your home. I know that makes you sad."

"It does." Mike thought about his orderly little apartment with the electronic gadgets, the well-stocked kitchen, the washer and dryer, the pillowtop mattress. He thought about his job. It could be annoying at times, but mostly he liked it. Liked it a lot. He got tremendous satisfaction out of the work he did, and he felt valued and appreciated for it. He thought about his friends. Jeff and Cleve and several other people he got together with regularly for card games or ball games or sometimes just to hang out. He thought about the bars he visited now and then, where he'd have a few drinks and find someone to fuck. And he thought about his family. His mom, who could be irritating as hell but who always supported him, no matter what. And Marie. She used to boss him around and torment him when they were kids, but by the time they grew up, they discovered they were friends.

But… what if he'd never been zapped to this place? He was having adventures other people couldn't even dream of, and at the side of the hottest guy he'd ever met. Mike missed home very much, but he couldn't regret having been brought here.

"Still no waterworks," Mike said, opening his eyes. "I told you. I'm just not built like that. I'm like the Grinch—heart two sizes too small. I don't let anything really touch me."

Goran scooted an inch or two closer so their knees touched. His skin looked golden in the candlelight, his hair like black silk. "Who told you that, Mike? Who made you believe that lie about yourself?"

"Nobody. I just—" Mike stopped under Goran's fierce glare. After a long moment, he muttered, "Benny."

"What?"

"That's his name: Benny. We met in college. We didn't start dating then because I was too busy and he was seeing someone else, but we were in a study group together. And I lusted over him. He was really handsome. He was like every jock fantasy I ever had in high school, all grown up." Well, mostly grown up. Benny had an appealing boyish quality well into his twenties.

Mike wondered if their priest had grown bored and wandered away yet. Poor girl. Did she want to be a priest when she was growing up, or was it something she got stuck with? Did it pay well? Did she have to be celibate?

"Mike?"

"Yeah. Sorry. So Benny and I lost touch after we graduated. But about a year later, we ran into each other at the grocery store. We were both comparison pricing breakfast cereals." He smiled at the memory. "So we met for coffee. Turned out he was single and so was I, and we started seeing each other."

"Seeing each other. Does that mean fucking?"

That caused Mike to laugh. "Yep. But more than that. We dated. Went out to dinners and movies and clubs. Hung out at each other's apartments. Spent most of our free time together. We even did the meet-the-parents thing."

"Did you love him, Mike?"

After pausing for a moment, Mike nodded. "I did. We were serious about each other. We talked about the future."

"Did you plan to get married?"

"Not exactly. We couldn't at the time. It wasn't allowed."

Goran's brow furrowed. "Why not?"

"Because we were both guys."

"What difference does that make if you love each other?"

"None as far as I'm concerned. But a lot of people seem to think it's important."

"That's stupid!"

Mike couldn't help a small grin at Goran's outrage. He wondered whether all alternate universes favored marriage equality, or if he'd just been lucky to get dumped in one that did. "It is stupid. Things are changing now back home too, but it's been a battle."

Goran nodded. "Good. If you could have married him, would you?"

"I thought so. I sure as hell wasn't seeing anyone else, and we talked sometimes about moving in together. Benny was kind of pushing for it, actually. But right about then, my dad got sick, and I was really busy with my new job and… it was too much all at once, I guess." Benny hadn't thought so. They'd argued about it, Benny pointing out how much time and money they were wasting with two apartments. But Mike had been gun-shy. Benny was the first man he'd ever fallen in love with, and Mike didn't want to screw things up by making quick decisions. Yeah, that had worked out *really* well.

"You don't like to be pushed," Goran said. "You like to be in control."

"I… yeah." He had been called a control freak more than once—often by Benny.

"What happened?"

"Nothing. Not for a while. We fought a lot, but in between we had makeup sex, and we had fun together. Maybe I should have known something was seriously wrong, but I didn't want to deal with it. Whenever Benny tried to have a serious talk, I ducked the subject. I was chickenshit."

"You were frightened."

Mike remembered the nights he'd spent tossing and turning alone in his bed, worrying about his dad and worrying about whether he was doing okay at work. And yes, scared to death he was losing Benny.

He cleared his throat. "It was my fault. Benny kept trying to talk to me…. When Dad died, Benny was great. He knew Dad didn't like him much, but Ben never said a bad thing about him, and he seemed really sorry Dad was gone. It meant a lot to me. Plus Benny never complained about all the time I had to spend at the hospital before that. He said he understood why I was distracted. He eased up on the moving-in thing too.

"But he started in again maybe six months after Dad died. He was really mad at me. Frustrated. But he told me he loved me anyway. God, he even suggested counseling. I got pissed off and told him we didn't need it. Last thing I wanted to do was talk about feelings in front of a stranger."

Mike's throat hurt—the smoke from the candles, maybe—and he found it difficult to talk. He wished he had some water, or better yet, ale. He wished Goran wasn't sitting there with compassion and sadness all over his handsome face. He wished… shit.

He rubbed his eyes with his fingertips. "Benny got sort of distant. We still spent a lot of time together and talked all the time, but not about anything important. We'd discuss work, sports, things like that. He stopped pushing me to move in with him. I was relieved about that. Oh hell, no, I wasn't. I was terrified. And it got even worse when he started having all these excuses about why we couldn't get together. Working late. Family stuff. Car troubles."

"He was lying."

"He was fucking around. Quite a bit, as it turned out. But mostly with one particular guy, and then only with one particular guy. Someone he met at the goddamn gym."

Mike laughed at the absurdity of it, at the ridiculous cliché. Except the laugh came out wrong, all twisted and harsh, tearing at his lungs. His jaw felt tight and his eyes burned. And fuck if he wasn't bawling like a baby.

Goran moved closer and wrapped his arms tightly around Mike, who promptly sobbed even harder, getting his tears and snot all over

Goran's only tunic. "I l-l-loved him," Mike cried against Goran's chest. "I r-really did. But he said I was too c-cold, and he broke my heart. Broke. It."

Goran didn't tell him he was stupid to cry over such a small thing. Didn't say that Mike had asked for it by refusing to discuss things openly with Benny. Didn't say it was no big deal. He simply held Mike tightly and smoothed his hair and back.

"Don't forget your tears," Goran whispered after a while.

Bleary-eyed, Mike pulled away. It took him a moment to figure out what Goran was talking about, and then he managed to laugh and sob at the same time—a weird sort of hiccup that hurt. He used Goran's shoulders to push himself to his feet, then walked the few feet to the center of the room. He ran two fingers over his wet cheeks, wiped the moisture on the inside of the glass bowl, and snuffled loudly. "I hope that's enough."

Goran came to his side and wound an arm around him. "Benny was wrong, Mike."

"No." Mike shook his head slowly. "I *am* a cold bastard. Since Ben I haven't really dated anyone. Haven't spent more than a few nights with anyone."

"Except me."

Mike looked up at Goran and almost broke out into fresh sobs. Because he was in love with Goran—as deeply and completely as he had been with Benny. More so. And it wasn't because Goran was so beautiful, although that wasn't exactly a hardship. It was Goran's kindness and loyalty that he loved, his cheerful willingness to do whatever was necessary without complaining. Mike loved how Goran let himself be bossed around and yet managed to care for them both so ably. Mike loved how Goran made him feel safe and smart and interesting.

Goddammit.

AFTER THE temple, they stopped for a meal—flaky spiral-shaped pastries filled with meat and veggies—and they both drank a great deal of ale. The sun was about to set and the streets were full of people as they walked back to their shed.

"Do you think that priest listened in while we were in the shrine?" Mike asked.

"Maybe," answered Goran. "Does it matter?"

"No. I guess the poor girl should get her entertainment where she can."

"Are you ashamed that you cried? You shouldn't be. Losing someone you love is… very difficult."

For a minute, Mike thought Goran was going to say more. But he remained silent all the way to their makeshift home. They didn't make love that night, but as usual they squished together on the bed. Mike tried to memorize all the physical aspects of Goran's closeness: the firm strength of his body, his warm breath tickling Mike's neck, the smell of his skin.

Chapter 12

MIKE WOKE up before Goran, which was unusual. The sun wasn't yet visible over the city walls and rooftops, but the stars had dimmed away as the sky began to brighten. Mike conducted his usual morning routine and dressed in his rattier set of clothing. He folded the nicer ones around the sandals and tucked them into a leather rucksack he'd asked Goran to buy. He added a few other items too—cheese, dried fruit, and nuts; a glass wine bottle filled with water and stoppered by a bit of cork; his little collection of toiletries. He was just shouldering the sack when Goran woke up.

"Ready to go?" Goran asked over a yawn. "You're eager to leave Varesh."

"I want to get this over with."

Goran stood and stretched hugely. His nude body was magnificent. "Just give me a few minutes and I'll be ready too."

Mike took a deep breath. "You're not going."

Goran blinked at him. "Pardon?"

"You're not going. You can stay here—you've got a pretty good gig with your job, especially with only one mouth to feed. Or you can move on. Whatever you want."

"But—"

"Here's the book." Mike pulled it from his vest and tried to hand it to Goran, who wouldn't take it. He set it on the table instead. "I've read over the damn thing a bunch of times now. I have only two more shrines anyway, and the ass-hat author doesn't say how to get there. I can ask along the way. I hope you get a lot of money for the damn thing."

"I don't understand. We're not finished with the pilgrimage yet."

"*I'm* not finished, you mean." Maybe if he talked really fast, this whole scene would be done quickly and with less accrued pain. Like ripping off a Band-Aid. "I can manage just fine from now on. I know how to beg people for food and shelter, and I know how to find berries and stuff on my own. I'm cool. I've even got these great boots you bought me. I'm just gonna cruise right through these last two shrines and I'm golden—home sweet home. And I'm sorry I can't pay you extra because man, you've totally earned it. But I guess this is a little bonus, right?" Now he pulled his blue briefs from his pocket and set them on top of the book. "They're clean. Um, maybe you can figure out the elastic thing and earn a fortune off that."

Goran slowly shook his head. "Why are you doing this? Did I do something wrong?"

"No. Of course not. You're… you're fucking perfect, Gor. But you've already done way more than you signed up for."

"I don't care. I don't care about your book or your… underwear either. I care about you, Mike!"

No no no. Not what he wanted to hear. Mike tried to walk to the door, but Goran stepped quickly, blocking his way. Mike considered just rushing him, but even naked and unarmed, Goran would easily win any fight. Mike resorted to words instead. "Let me go!"

"No! You're not making any sense. Are you feeling ill?"

"I feel fine. Dammit, Goran! I'm not an invalid. I'm not a pretty little helpless boy. I might not be"—he gestured vaguely in Goran's direction—"Hercules… but I am capable of taking care of myself. I don't need you."

Goran recoiled a little as if he'd been hit. But he didn't budge from the door. "What are you scared of, Mike?"

"Nothing!" Mike roared. "I had my goddamn meltdown yesterday, but now I'm fine."

"All right. You're fine. You can take care of yourself. But don't you still want my company?" Goran was making a visible effort to keep himself calm.

So Mike tried to tone it down too. Hysterical didn't suit him. "I've lied to you, Goran. I've kept secrets from you—big ones. And I've used you. I'm going to finish my errands, and then I'm going to go home, and you can't go with me. It's just not possible. And... Jesus, Gor. I'm not Pavo. I'm not cute and smart and capable and... and all that. I'm an asshole. A selfish asshole. That whole thing with Benny blew up because I refused to talk straight with him, so now I'm talking straight with you. I can't do this. Do... us." His eyes stung again, a fresh round of tears threatening to erupt.

Goran was crying. Big, fat tears coursed down his cheeks, making him look vulnerable and wounded but not ugly, never ugly. His voice was hoarse. "But Mike, I lo—"

"Don't. Please. Just don't." He couldn't look Goran in the eyes anymore, so he stared at a random spot a few feet to the left. "Let me go, Goran."

Looking like he wanted to kill someone, Goran stepped aside.

Mike didn't say another word. Didn't turn for one last look as he crossed the yard. Didn't allow a single tear to escape. He'd made the right decision.

"You have a fucking lot to answer for, Agata," he muttered. And he headed for the nearest city gate.

Chapter 13

THE NEXT-TO-LAST shrine was somewhere called Obrov. The guidebook author had told Mike that much, along with a recipe for soothing eye drops, a bawdy tale about a farmer's daughters and a sailor, and advice on the best time of year for planting barley. Mike asked a man selling eggs where Obrov was. The man just glared at him silently, but an old woman browsing at the next market stall overheard. "It's northwest of here," she said. "Just follow the Tanis River. You can take a boat and be there tomorrow."

"I don't have money for a boat."

"Then walk along the river road. Three days, maybe four."

He smiled at her. "Thank you."

"You're a pilgrim?"

"Yes."

"Made a pilgrimage myself when I was a girl. Not to Obrov, though. I wanted to beg Agata for children."

Mike managed to suppress a scowl at the goddess's name. "How did that work out?"

She grinned toothlessly at him. "I had eight!"

The Tanis was the widest of the four rivers in Varesh, the one with the most boat traffic. One evening Goran had showed Mike the docks where he worked—broad wooden platforms where dozens of small craft were tethered and where men and women swarmed like ants. It was a little too early this morning for the loading and unloading to begin, but there was still activity as people cleaned the docks and ships and as carts queued up alongside the river, waiting for cargo transfer. Donkeys brayed irritably, humans laughed and argued as they munched their breakfasts or drank their ale. Mike walked past them all, his heart aching.

He'd made the right choice.

Soon he passed through the unguarded city gate and then alongside the modest houses that sprawled outside the city walls. Hens clucked at him and dogs barked. The air was warm already, but the river looked clean and fresh. His boots were really fucking comfortable.

As he continued walking, the houses became more widely scattered and fields and orchards flourished between them. There was little other foot traffic, but sometimes a boat would float by. Mike wished he'd been able to afford to ride one. He'd always liked traveling by water. He and Benny even went on a cruise together once—they'd taken the Inside Passage to Skagway. They'd spent hours sitting in the hot tub, watching eagles fly overhead as the ship drifted past glaciers. They'd talked about doing a longer cruise in the future. Somewhere warm maybe, or perhaps one of those European river cruises. It never happened.

Deciding to save his food supplies for later, Mike begged lunch from a pair of middle-aged women who were weeding their front garden. Unlike Goran, he couldn't do any tasks in return. So he simply thanked them before continuing on his way.

Later he got dinner from a young family and spent the night in their barn. A cow occupied the stall next to his. She wasn't bad company, for a cow. He had college roommates who were noisier and smellier. But gods, he missed having Goran sleeping at his side.

Roosters woke him in the morning, and he resumed his walking. He didn't have much to occupy his thoughts—the road was straight and even, the scenery unremarkable—so despite his best efforts, he kept thinking about Goran. He remembered the little songs Goran liked to sing and the way he liked to tease Mike good-naturedly until Mike couldn't help but laugh. Goran knew the names of all the plants they passed, all the birds and animals. One night when they were in the forest, a sudden storm brought heavy sheets of rain, and together they pulled down tree branches to build a makeshift shelter. By then they were soaked to the skin, so they stripped and huddled together, listening to the downpour and fooling around until their hearts beat louder than thunder and their pleasure crackled like lightning.

Leaving Goran was the right thing to do. Additional time together would only prolong the pain for both of them, would only imply promises about a future they could never have.

Goran talked in his sleep sometimes. Mike could never quite make out the words, but Goran always seemed distressed, moaning and flinching and twitching his hands. Whenever this happened, Mike pulled him closer and smoothed the hair away from his face, and Goran would soon slip back into peaceful slumber. Would he soon find someone else to ease his nightmares?

Goran was a big boy. Really big. He was certainly more than capable of taking care of himself.

When Mike was by himself in towns, nobody spared him a second glance. Goran, though—people couldn't help but notice him. Both men and women stared in awestruck lust. But Goran pretended they didn't exist. His entire attention was on Mike, as if Mike were the most fascinating person in the world. In two worlds.

Goran, handsome and capable and sweet, would surely have no trouble finding another lover right away, if he were so inclined. He could find someone better suited to him—a strong, outdoorsy type, maybe, or some rich man who could give him a comfortable home.

Mike's thoughts continued this way all day until he was so sick of his own company he was ready to hurl himself into the river. He didn't even have hunger or thirst or aching feet to distract him: his boots were great, and there were numerous small hamlets along the road where he could find someone to feed him. An MP3 player would have been wonderful. He could have played something really loud and not remotely angsty or lovelorn. AC/DC. Black Sabbath.

He covered a lot of ground, so determined about marching on and so caught up in his head that he was still walking after sundown. This was not a good idea. Goran had warned him that outside of cities, the main roads weren't safe at night. Bandits, he said. Outlaws. And not, Mike had the impression, the sexy antihero sorts of outlaws with chaps and bandanas and scruffy beards, who turned out to be wrongly accused and unjustly persecuted, and to have hearts of gold. No,

Nenahde had *real* bad guys who'd managed to escape the pillar and the noose and who had nothing to lose by robbing and murdering travelers.

So Mike probably shouldn't have been surprised when, at a spot where the road squeezed between the river and a thick copse, three people leapt out to block his way.

With his heart pounding, Mike reviewed every piece of advice he'd ever heard about what to do if faced with a mugging. Hand everything over. Don't be a hero. Try to get the attention of passersby.

"Out for a stroll?" asked one of the trio pleasantly. Mike realized with a start that it was a woman, obscured by the dark and shrouded by a cloak and hood.

He tried a polite smile. "Just about to head in for the night."

"Really? The nearest inn is over an hour from here."

"I… I was going to walk faster. So if you'll excuse me—"

"What's in your sack?" That was one of the others, a tall man with a gruff voice and a slight lisp.

"Nothing. Just a change of clothes. Look. I'm on a pilgrimage. I have absolutely nothing of value. Not even a single leeka."

"Which god are you honoring?" asked the woman.

"Alina."

All three of them laughed, and not in a nice way. They came a few steps closer. "That's excellent," said the woman. "You can become your own offering to the god of death."

Fuck. But Mike wasn't panicking. He was terrified, yes, but his head remained clear. "I'll give you my pack, okay? You can have whatever you want. There's no need for you to kill me."

"No need, maybe," said the woman, "but no reason not to. I owe Alina a gift in any case."

Mike couldn't get past them. Dense shrubbery blocked his way to the right, and to the left was the cold and swift-flowing river. He did fine paddling around in a swimming pool or a pond, but he wasn't an especially strong swimmer. Besides, the guy with the lisp was close enough that he could make a grab for Mike if he tried to dive in. And that left only retreat. He could turn, run, and hope he was faster than these three and didn't trip over a rock in the dark and fall on his face.

Faster *and* with better endurance, because the last sign of habitation had been a long way back.

Now the outlaws were so close Mike could smell them. Personal hygiene apparently wasn't a priority. He took a few steps backward, and they slowly followed him.

"I don't think we should kill him right away," said the third person, speaking for the first time. Male, and the bulkiest of the three. "I think we should play with him awhile first."

"You always think with your dick first," the woman said, chuckling.

The tall guy chimed in, "That's because his dick's bigger than his brain."

Mike felt sick. It had never before occurred to him to fear rape. He backed up a little more, followed closely by the trio. The man who thought with his dick reached out and stroked Mike's face. Mike knocked his hand away, which made the others laugh. "Come on, pilgrim. Let me show you what a real man's cock is like. Might just fuck you to death instead of slitting your throat."

Good gods. Were perverted bullying shitheads the same in every world? Mike growled like a pit bull. "Keep your fucking hands to yourself and get out of my way." He swung the rucksack off his shoulders so it hung in front of him, and he reached inside.

"Are you going to fight us with your spare clothing, pilgrim?" taunted the would-be rapist.

Mike didn't answer. Instead, he pulled out the bottle, dropped the pack, and scurried backward a bit more. He crouched just long enough to shatter the bottle against the hard-packed dirt, then stood again, jagged glass held outward. "Make my day," he snarled.

All three of his opponents pulled knives. The blades glinted in the moonlight. Fine. He was going to go down fighting and do as much damage as possible while he was at it. The woman swiped at him; he jabbed back and was very satisfied when he felt the glass dig into her shoulder. She yelped and jumped back.

But before Mike could feel victorious, the two men were after him. One of them stabbed Mike's lower right arm. It hurt like hell, but

Mike managed to hold on to the bottle. The other aimed for Mike's face, scoring a nasty gash on his cheek but fortunately missing his eye.

As quickly as everything was moving, Mike's head stayed remarkably clear. He was going to die. And he wasn't going to die in a car wreck or of cancer or by any of the other ways he'd thought likely. He was going to get hacked to pieces by outlaws on a lonely road in an alternate universe while midway through a pilgrimage. "I don't even *read* fantasy!" he yelled. And he laughed at the absurdity of it all. But he wasn't afraid anymore, and that was good.

All three attackers surged forward at once. Mike retreated, bottle waving. And just when he thought he might survive a few minutes longer and inflict a few more wounds, heavy running footsteps sounded behind him. He heard the very distinctive sound of a sword being drawn from its scabbard. He prepared himself for the sensation of steel biting through his neck or plunging through his back—

But instead a heavy sword came down on the rapist's knife arm, severing it completely. A lot of screaming and shouting ensued, a lot of scuffling that was very confusing in the darkness. Mike remained right in the middle of it, moving without really thinking. He didn't come back to himself until he was on his knees, plunging his broken bottle into a lifeless body. A large hand grasped his shoulder, urging him up. "It's all right," said a calm, familiar voice. "They're dead."

"G-Goran?"

"You're hurt. Let me—"

"Goran? What are you— How…?"

Instead of answering, Goran pushed him gently back against the edge of the thicket. As Mike watched, Goran sheathed his sword after a cursory wipe, then tossed each of the corpses into the river. Even though he was breathing heavily from the fight, Goran handled the heavy bodies easily, as if they were nothing but cargo to be offloaded. Then he turned and wrapped an arm around Mike's shoulders. Mike didn't resist as Goran urged him along the road a short way to a small meadow.

"Sit," ordered Goran, pushing at Mike's shoulders.

"But—"

"Sit."

Mike sat. More heavily than he'd intended, really. And only when he was seated did he realize he was still clutching the bottle. His fingers had locked in place like a vise, and he had to will them to release; the bottle thudded to the soft ground.

Goran took off at a trot. Mike shook his head, wondering if he was dying on the road and hallucinating the rest, but then Goran came running back with an armload of twigs. He dumped them on the ground, and in a remarkably short time, he had a fire going.

He hissed when he saw the slice on Mike's face, and then again when he rolled up Mike's sleeve. "You're hurt," he repeated.

"I'm— What the hell is going on?" Mike knew he sounded more plaintive than demanding.

"I'm patching you up." Goran rummaged in a small sack tied to his belt. "I decided after Ugolin that I should be prepared if I was going to travel with you. Good thing." He pulled out a handful of dried leaves, pressed them to the wound in Mike's arm, and tied a strip of cloth as bandage. Then he tended to the cut on Mike's face, cleaning it with a damp cloth he'd acquired somehow, followed by dabbing with more leaves. After that he washed the bandits' blood from Mike's hand.

"You're going to have more scars," Goran said with a sigh.

"Then I won't be a pretty boy anymore."

Goran managed a small smile. "Yes, you will. Always."

"Gor, what the hell?"

"I was… following you."

Yeah, that was fairly clear. "For how long?"

"Since you left Varesh."

"You've been following me for two days?"

"I'm a hunter, Mike. And I'm… I know how to keep myself hidden if I want to." He drew his sword and began to meticulously clean the blade with a cloth, checking the edges in preparation for honing.

"Why were you stalking me? Because you knew I'd do something stupid?"

Goran didn't look at him. "Because I love you. I didn't want to lose you."

Shit.

"I'm sorry I wasn't faster, Mike. They… they almost killed you."

"But they didn't. They—" Mike stopped as he had a sudden sense memory of grinding broken glass into a soft and vulnerable throat. "What happened?"

"I killed two of them. The other was yours. You were very brave, Mike."

Mike's laugh had an edge of hysteria. "Brave? I didn't even— didn't even know what I was doing. I…. Fuck." He sank his face into his hands, which was a mistake—it hurt both his cheek and his arm. He felt a little shaky and decided that lying down was a very good idea. So he did, but even then he felt the earth spinning beneath him.

Goran sheathed the sword and hurried over. "Mike? Are you all right?"

"Just… a little overwhelmed here. I *murdered* someone. Jesus. I feel grossed out when I squish spiders in my bathtub."

"You killed someone who was trying to harm you. You killed to survive. There's no shame in that."

"Does this place recognize self-defense? Are we going to end up with the noose?"

"Mike." Goran stroked Mike's uninjured cheek very gently, like he might pet a timid kitten. "They were outlaws. Even if they hadn't attacked, you could have killed them without fear of punishment. That's what being an outlaw means."

"Oh." Mike closed his eyes for a moment, but that made the spinning worse. What seemed to help most was looking up into Goran's face, concentrating on Goran's touch.

"Are you going to be all right, Mike? Even if you had no choice, even if it was the right thing to do… taking another life hurts. It leaves scars inside."

Mike thought about that for a moment. "You've killed before, haven't you? More than once."

Goran sighed. "Yes."

"Tell me."

"It's late and you're wounded. You've had a terrible day. Let's sleep and—"

"*Tell* me." In a softer voice, Mike added, "I don't want to sleep. Not yet. I'm remembering the sound a throat makes when it's impaled by a broken bottle."

Goran caressed Mike's jaw. "All right. But give me a minute." Before Mike could answer, he'd stood and run off again. He returned quickly with Mike's rucksack. Mike had forgotten all about it. Goran slipped it under Mike's head as a pillow and then spent several more minutes fussing with him: making him drink from the water skin, arranging him more comfortably on the ground, adding more wood to the fire. Finally he seemed to run out of excuses, and he sat next to Mike, not quite touching him. Mike reached out and laced his fingers with Goran's.

"Pavo and I... when we first got to Strazha, we lived however we could. He was quick, so sometimes he stole things. Sometimes we begged or scavenged. Sometimes... sometimes we sold ourselves."

"Jesus, Gor." Seeing the stricken look on Goran's face, Mike squeezed his hand. "No child should have to go through that. I'm sorry."

"We survived. I was always big for my age, and soon I was big enough for a man's job. I'd haul heavy loads, help dig and repair roads. It wasn't as good as hunting, but it was honest work. Pavo was a runner."

"What's that?"

"He ran errands. Delivering goods for merchants, carrying messages for rich people, that sort of thing. Also honest work. He had plans. We would save enough money to buy a stable. Maybe an old one that needed repairs—I could do that. He could care for people's horses and I could help. He talked about it all the time. I think he dreamed about it."

"It sounds like a good plan."

Goran nodded but remained silent for a while, staring over Mike and into the flames. There were smudges of blood on his face and splatters on his neck and tunic. Most of his hair had escaped from the ponytail. "It was a good plan," he said finally. "But it wasn't mine."

Mike waited. He squeezed Goran's hand again. Could you transfer emotional strength via fingertips the same way you transferred body heat?

"I wanted revenge, Mike. I wanted to kill the people who murdered my father and stole my home. Pavo told me I was foolish, told me to forget it and move on. He married me. Said now we were our own family and that was good enough. We fought about it. Often. Until one day Pavo gave in. You might have noticed that I'm a little stubborn." He tried a smile, which made Mike's heart ache.

Mike remembered how he'd felt when he'd been crying his eyes out in the Temple of Four Winds and Goran had held him so tightly. So he managed to lever himself into a sitting position. And then—dignity be damned—he crawled right into Goran's lap. "What happened?" he whispered against Goran's neck.

Goran wrapped his arms around Mike's body. "We left Strazha. We went to the lord who killed my father—to his castle. But it's not so easy for people like us to get close to a great lord like him. We decided—no, I decided to become one of his men-at-arms. His captain was glad to have someone big and strong like me. Pavo they weren't so pleased with at first, but then they saw his skill with horses."

"So you became soldiers."

"Among the very men who'd destroyed our home, yes. And we fought, because that's what soldiers do. This lord wasn't satisfied with taking over my home—he was trying to conquer all the small lords around him. I think he wanted to be king."

"Can you do it that way?" Mike was uncertain about royal politics in his own world, let alone here. "Do you get to be king if you beat enough opponents?" Like playing Risk, maybe.

"I don't know. He thought so. And while I waited to get close enough to assassinate him, we fought his battles. I killed... I killed." Goran's breath caught for a moment, and then he let it out loudly, slowly. "I killed men who were trying to protect their homes, their families."

Mike didn't point out that those people probably would have died even if Goran had never become a soldier; some other soldier would have killed them instead. Even though it was true, it wouldn't change the way Goran felt. Not any more than knowing he was defending himself from rape and murder changed the way Mike felt. "I'm sorry," he said again.

"They still haunt me in my sleep, Mike. Their faces… their children crying and cowering."

Mike allowed him to sit in silence for a while. The fire crackled and snapped. "Is that how you got all the scars, Gor?"

Goran shuddered slightly. "Yes."

And Mike knew that Goran's shame and embarrassment over the scars wasn't over the marks themselves but rather how he'd earned them. "You must have been badly injured more than once."

"Yes. But I always survived." He was quiet again for a long time, and then in a tiny, raspy voice, he added, "Pavo didn't."

"Oh, Goran."

"I killed him. Might as well have run him through with a sword myself. Gods, if we'd stayed in Strazha like he wanted to…." He sobbed only once, and his voice was steady as he continued. "I was at his side when he died. He said not to blame myself. Said it was fate. Told me to find someone to love.

"And you know what? I kept on fighting. I was even more convinced I had to kill that lord—it was his fault too that my Pavo was dead. A few weeks later I had a chance. We were traveling. I slipped into his tent at night and cut his throat. He never made a sound. It wasn't…. I didn't feel anything. I wasn't happy he was dead.

"I left that night, and I've been traveling ever since. Over ten years. I used to worry that if I stayed too long, someone might recognize me as the man who killed that lord. Then I just got in the habit. I've hired myself out as a guard, earned enough to buy more ale. Because if I drink enough ale, I can silence those voices for a little while." Goran snorted. "I've killed more men since, but only while protecting others. I don't know if that's any better."

"It was tonight, Gor. You saved my life."

Goran squeezed him. "*That* was worth it. I'd kill a thousand men to save you."

"Hopefully that won't be necessary."

"You know what, Mike? You silence the voices too. When I'm near you, I feel… worthy. I feel like there's a reason to go on. That's why I followed you."

Mike wanted to cry again. "But I told you. I can't take you with me. I want to. I… I really want to. Remember how Benny said I wouldn't let him in? You're in, dammit. In here." Mike pulled away enough to pound a fist against his heart. His right fist. Ouch. "But you have to believe me, Gor. It's just not possible." He very nearly divulged his last secret but bit his tongue. He couldn't afford to piss off Agata.

"I know," Goran said quietly. "But we can have a little more time together, can't we? I'd have given anything for just a few days more with Pavo. Let me have them with you."

"It's not like I could get rid of you even if I wanted to, now could I?" Mike leaned in close and kissed Goran's bloody cheek.

Chapter 14

THEY DIDN'T travel far the next day. Goran was worried about Mike's wounds and wanted to play healer. The throbbing cuts were annoying, but alone they were not enough to keep Mike from walking. He was tired, though. Somehow getting jumped, killing someone, and listening to his lover spill his guts took a lot out of him. Mike was willing to take it easy for a day. At the next village, Goran splurged on a room at an inn, using some of his wages from Varesh. The river route attracted those traveling by foot and by boat, and most of them had the good sense to put in somewhere safe for the night. Consequently, each village offered several inns, and enough competition that some of them were fairly decent. They got a private room with a big bed covered in clean linens. The landlady scowled at Mike's wounds and Goran's bloodstained clothing, but then Goran said a single word—"Bandits"—and her demeanor changed. She fussed over them both, making sure they had a big lunch with lots of ale and promising to clean their dirty clothes. She even had her two sons carry up a large copper tub and several buckets of hot water, so Mike had the luxury of a warm bath.

Once Mike was clean, Goran tended to his wounds. The landlady had given them a viscous stinky ointment, which Goran smeared liberally onto Mike's damaged skin. And of course Goran made Mike drink gallons of that terrible tea. The more faces Mike pulled over the vile stuff, the more satisfied Goran looked.

After Mike was cleaned and stuffed and rubbed and medicated, Goran tucked him into bed even though it wasn't yet dinnertime. "Rest," he ordered.

"You too." Mike patted the mattress.

"After everything I told you, you still want—"

"I still want. But right now I'd just like to sleep with you, okay? I was too out of it to enjoy last night."

For the first time since they'd reunited, Goran flashed his sunny smile. He stripped off his belt, boots, and trousers—his tunic was already in the landlady's hands—and he climbed in beside Mike. Even though they had plenty of room, they squashed together, Goran wrapping himself around Mike's back. Then they sighed in unison.

"Are you all right, Mike?"

"Yeah. And let me sleep, 'cause after all that tea, pretty soon I'm gonna need to wake up and take a piss."

Goran chuckled and tickled Mike's side, but then he settled down with a soft contented grunt.

MIKE DID need to piss when he woke up. Badly. Goran was still snoring comfortably, so Mike moved very slowly out from under the covers and off the bed. There was a chamber pot in a cabinet. As he used it, he admitted how much he missed plumbing. If he ever got home, he'd never again take a toilet for granted.

He was less stealthy getting back into bed, causing Goran to stir and mumble sleepily. "Dinnertime?"

Mike patted his lover's flat belly. "Not yet, big guy. Go back to sleep." Through the open window he could hear sounds from the kitchen below: the homey clatter of pots and pans and the friendly banter between the landlady and another woman.

Goran embraced him from behind as usual, but it was immediately clear that sleeping was not foremost on his mind. His cock was hard, pressing into the crack of Mike's ass. Mike chuckled and pushed himself back more firmly.

"Is this all right?' Goran asked. "Are you well enough?"

"I'm not a delicate flower, Gor. As long as you stay away from my face and right arm, I'll be just fine."

He received in reply a snuffle at the crook of his neck and a big hand reaching around to fondle his balls. "You feel so good against me, Mike." A swipe of hot tongue on his shoulder. "You smell good too."

"Good enough to eat?"

"Delicious." Goran settled Mike onto his back and shoved the covers away so he could nestle his head where Mike's leg met his torso. Mike was already rock hard—he'd never before felt so turned on so quickly. But Goran was cruel—instead of sucking Mike off, he licked at the crease of Mike's leg, gently mouthed his scrotum, fucked his navel with his tongue.

Mike had to stop himself from whining. He grabbed double handfuls of Goran's hair and tried to use it as reins to urge his head into the right position. Goran chuckled. "Is there something you want, Mike?"

"You. Want you."

That must have been the right answer, because Goran kissed the tip of Mike's cock before sliding the crown between his lips. Mike had found that Goran wasn't the most skilled giver of blowjobs he'd ever met, but what he lacked in skill he made up for in enthusiasm. And really, just the sight of him between Mike's legs—every ounce of his attention wrapped up in making Mike feel good—that was better than being deep-throated. Goran had already learned what Mike liked, and so as he sucked and licked, he also inserted a spit-slicked finger into Mike's ass.

"Fuck, fuck, fuck, fuck…." Mike realized he was chanting loudly—and the window was open. He wondered whether the landlady was enjoying the entertainment. And then he didn't care because Goran was delicately tonguing his slit while rubbing his prostate just right.

"Gonna— Gor, stop— Gonna—"

Goran did stop, and not a moment too soon. He looked up at Mike with wild eyes, the pupils almost obscuring the green irises. He scooted up until his torso was aligned with Mike's, his hand plenty large enough to grip both cocks at once. Together they writhed and moaned. A thousand outlaws could have burst into the room just then, followed by a thousand angry gods, and Mike still couldn't have stopped. His orgasm was like a neurological tsunami, so pure and fierce that it was almost agony.

Goran collapsed on top of him, which would have made it hard for Mike to breathe if his lungs had been working. They weren't. None of him worked—he'd blown a full-body fuse.

"You killed me," Goran groaned after a few moments. He rolled to the side, flopped onto his back, and lay there panting.

"Ditto. That was... good gods, Gor."

"It's because of last night. Brushes with death always make life more... real. Because Agata and Alina are sisters. Can't have one without the other."

"I thought you said they don't get along."

"They don't. But they need each other too, and they both know it. So they play little games with each other. Like children kicking a ball around—and humans are the ball. One time Agata might score a small victory and Alina the next, but neither will ever defeat the other."

Mike remembered what a baseball looked like after a good game with lots of hits: dirty, torn, misshapen. That's the kind of ball he felt like. But hey, he was still in the game.

THE LANDLADY and her sons giggled when Mike and Goran appeared for dinner, which made Mike blush hotly. Goran only smirked. When the landlady plopped their plates down in front of them, she said, "I've given you some extra meat. To help you recover from your... exertions." That sent her sons and Goran into gales of laughter. Mike wanted to crawl under the table.

But he soon forgot his embarrassment. The food was good and plentiful, and the ale was some of the best he'd found. The company wasn't bad either. The landlady, her family, and the locals had apparently decided Mike and Goran were minor heroes, which meant the visitors were cheerfully included in the discussion and laughter.

Goran didn't drink enough to get drunk, but he looked relaxed and happy. When the food was gone and a large bowl of berries and cream downed for dessert, he slung an arm around Mike's shoulders and joined some of the others in belting out several songs. It was like medieval karaoke. Mike did not chime in, but he had fun listening.

The hour was late when they returned to their room. Goran made Mike drink more tea, and rewarded him with a quick rubdown with a towel and warm water.

"These people like you, Gor," Mike said as they climbed into bed.

"They're good people."

"You could come back here after I'm gone. I'm sure you'd find some way to make a living. Keep the region bandit-free, maybe. You'd have friends. A home."

Goran sighed and shook his head. "I don't think so."

"Why not?"

"I told you. The… the voices. They'll return when you leave."

"So you'll just keep running away? You can't run from something that's in your head, Gor."

"I know."

Chapter 15

EVEN WITHOUT roosters they woke up early. Mike stood and stretched and began gathering his things. Goran watched him from the bed. "We can stay here another day, Mike. Let you heal a little more."

"I'm fine. A little achy around the wounds, but that's all. Besides, I don't want you spending all your money."

"Why not?"

"Because you could use it later."

Goran shrugged. "I'll only spend it on drink." Then he rose too.

The landlady insisted on sending them off with as much food as Mike could stuff in his rucksack, along with a jar of ointment for his wounds and clean strips of rags to use as bandages. "I hope you'll come back this way, boys. And when you do, you be sure to stay here at the White Hart."

Mike smiled at her. "We wouldn't think of staying anywhere else."

They stepped out into the bright morning. Goran pointed to a boat docked nearby. "We could take that instead of walking. I have enough coppers, and we could be in Obrov by lunch."

But now Mike wasn't in such a hurry for the pilgrimage to end. "Let's walk. I think it's better penance that way," he lied.

Goran returned Mike's grin.

It was so much nicer traveling with Goran than alone. Not just for the companionship and safety, although those things were good. But

Goran's presence made Mike feel that the world—this weird world he'd been zapped to—was spinning as it should. As if Goran were meant to be with him. Which was stupid, because Mike didn't believe in fate.

They camped out in the woods that night. They probably could have begged a spot in someone's barn, or Goran could have paid for another inn, but they preferred privacy. Mike had come to enjoy glimpses of stars through the leaves and falling asleep with the crickets, owls, and other forest creatures as his lullaby. Besides, no damn roosters in the morning.

By the middle of the next day, the terrain had changed, becoming hillier and drier. Sometimes the road traversed the top of substantial cliffs, with a sheer drop down to the Tanis River. From those heights, the passing boats looked like toys.

"It's like flying," Goran said as they rested at the crest of a particularly tall precipice, his feet dangling over the edge.

Mike kept himself back a safe distance. "I always love to watch the scenery when I fly. Reminds me of quilts."

Goran twisted around to gape at him. "When you *fly*?"

Shit. Mike tried to think of an explanation that would make sense to Goran. Giant metal machines that hurled through the air faster than the fastest birds, higher than any mountains, and with hundreds of people in their bellies? Yeah, that sounded credible.

"Are you a wizard, Mike?"

"Uh, no. Are there really wizards?"

"I didn't think so. I thought they were just stories." Goran frowned. "Are you… something else? A half god?"

"I'm just a man, Gor. Very ordinary."

"Nothing ordinary about you," Goran said, shaking his head. And thankfully, he let the flying thing go.

OBROV LAY in a narrow valley, at a spot where a smaller river merged with the Tanis. It was a very strange place. Without much level ground to inhabit, the locals had carved their homes right into the cliffside.

Some of these manmade caves looked large and elaborate, and they were reached by steep rock stairways that gave Mike vertigo just looking at them.

People here seemed to live primarily off fishing. Huge nets were submerged near the rivers' confluence. Men and women tugged them in, quickly picked out the catch they wanted, and dumped the rest back in, still alive and squirming.

A handsome shirtless man leered happily at Mike and Goran as they neared the cliff. "Welcome to Obrov!" he boomed. He was in his early twenties and very muscular, although not as much as Goran. "If you're planning to stay, I have room for you both." He pointed up at one of the cave houses, but his lascivious gaze made it clear he was hoping for something other than a few coins' payment.

Goran didn't look amused. "My master is on a pilgrimage," he said.

"To Alina's shrines?" The man spat to the side. "Waste of time. Agata offers much more enjoyable pastimes."

"I know. But he's dedicated to Alina now."

"Shame." The man turned as if to walk away.

Goran stopped him with a hand on the shoulder. "Can you tell us where the shrine is?"

"Fifteen minutes down the valley. You can't miss it. There's an enormous boulder taking up almost all the land. Do you know what happened there?"

Mike didn't really want to know, but he also didn't want to be rude. "What?"

"There was a huge cave—a natural one, not dug from the rock like ours. Once every four years, all the youths who'd recently come of age would spend a month living in that cave. It was supposed to help them learn to live on their own, and most of them would find mates that way too."

Mike nodded. Sort of a bar mitzvah, prom, and freshman dorm, all mixed up in one.

"A hundred years ago, a group of youths went to the cave. There were twelve of them. And the earth shook. A huge chunk of rock broke from the cliff above them and fell in front of the cave mouth, blocking it. Everyone in the village worked for weeks trying to save them, but they couldn't get through or around that rock. All twelve of them are still there. People say their ghosts haunt the valley."

"That's awful," Mike said with a shudder. He didn't want to imagine the horror of being entombed alive.

Goran asked, "Why make it a shrine to Alina?"

The man spat again. "She took them. Might as well give the bitch her due." His posture relaxed a little, and his crooked grin reappeared. "When you're done with her, come look for me. I promise you more fun than she can give you."

"Wait!" Mike said before the guy could walk away. "What am I supposed to offer her here?"

"Something truly valuable to you. Because she took what was most valuable from us." With a wave, the man walked off.

Mike didn't know what the secondary river was called, and he didn't ask. Whatever its name, the valley it had carved was more accurately a canyon. The river itself wasn't very big or fast, and it was hard to believe it had managed to dig so deeply into rock. But he'd been to the Grand Canyon once, and that was all done by a river too. The strength of water was amazing.

Nobody seemed to live in the canyon. Maybe floods were an issue, or maybe they just liked the wider spot where this smaller river met the Tanis. It was pretty terrain—the cliffsides stained in red-and-brown stripes, colorful wildflowers burrowing their roots into little crevices and outcroppings, birds riding the thermals high overhead. Occasionally, very narrow side canyons ran off at angles, most of them with a shallow stream that trickled into the river. Once an enormous animal darted out of one of the canyons, took a look at Mike and Goran, and hurried back to safety with an alarmed bray.

"What the hell was that?" asked Mike.

Goran laughed and clapped him on the back. "Bundabeast. They taste good, and their hides make good coats. But it'd be a huge waste to kill one just for the two of us."

"Are they dangerous?"

"No. You saw—they're terrified of everything. There's an old story about a bundabeast that saw its own reflection in a pool and dropped dead of fright."

"Oh." Bundabeast. Mike wondered if squirrels and sparrows would seem as exotic to Goran as the creatures of this world seemed to him. But then he chased that thought from his head. Goran would never get a chance to see Mike's world, and even if Mike were able to tell his secret, talking about it would only be a tease.

Their new friend had been right; the boulder was easy to spot. It was as big as Mike's old elementary school. The river had rerouted around the boulder, finding the path of least resistance against the opposite canyon wall. What would have happened if the boulder had dammed the river completely?

Twelve small statues had been set into the ground in a semicircle very close to the boulder. Each statue was about three feet tall and shaped vaguely like a person, but without a face or hands or feet. They were really creepy. In front of the semicircle was a small pile of debris. Mike could make out the glint of metal—coins or jewelry—and some folded cloth, but couldn't identify the rest.

"Here," Goran said. Mike turned and saw Goran holding out the book. "It's worth a lot of money, Mike. Even more than my sword."

"But it's yours. It's your payment."

Goran sighed noisily. "I don't want payment from you. Not anymore."

"Consider it a gift, then. Besides, that stupid book isn't worth jack shit to me. It's the most useless guidebook I've ever seen." And then a thought struck him. "Except if you hadn't seen me reading it, you wouldn't have asked me to hire you, would you?"

"Probably not."

"So it's extremely valuable," said Mike, earning a soft smile. But then he shook his head. "But it did its job weeks ago. Now I have no use for it."

"Then what will you give?"

Mike looked down at his feet unhappily. This was going to hurt.

"Not your boots!" Goran protested. "You can give my knife instead."

Goran was willing to allow himself to be half-disarmed so that Mike would have comfortable footwear? That wasn't a sacrifice Mike was willing to let him make. "I think it has to be something important to me, Gor," he said softly. "And the only important things I have here are my boots and you. And no way I'm giving you to Alina."

He sat on a handy rock and began to undo the boot toggles. He really should have shown the shoemaker how to do shoelaces.

"Wait," Goran said, hand on Mike's shoulder. He rummaged in the cloth sack at his waist and pulled out a small ball of blue fabric, which Mike recognized at once: his briefs. He held them out. "These."

"You think a god wants my used underwear?"

"They're the only thing you brought with you from California. You made sure to wash them every chance you got. I think you value them a great deal."

Mike thought about it. Damn if Goran wasn't right. Boots were replaceable. But if Mike never returned home, those briefs would be all he had of his original life.

He refastened his boot and stood, then took the underwear from Goran's outstretched hand. "Thanks. These are perfect."

Goran was his only witness, but Mike felt as if a dozen pairs of eyes watched as he walked into the space in front of the statues and set down the briefs. "They don't look like much," he said, addressing Alina. "But they're the only ones in this wor—in this place. They're comfy. I always thought they showed off my package and my ass pretty nicely. My mother gave them to me, and they're the only souvenir I have of home. So please accept this gift. And please forgive the wrong that was done to you."

That was as eloquent as he could be.

He and Goran discussed what to do next. The sensible thing would be to return to the village of Obrov and find a place to spend the night. Neither wanted to accept the offer of that handsome young man, but perhaps someone else could spare them a bed. In the end they decided to stay in the canyon. Mike couldn't explain why—and he knew he was being ridiculous—but he felt that sleeping near the shrine would help honor the memory of the twelve lost youths.

"You're not afraid of ghosts?" asked Goran.

"Don't believe in them. Besides, you'd protect me."

Goran grinned hugely.

They found a level spot near one of the cross-canyons. Goran built a fire, and they ate most of the food left over from the White Hart. Then they lay down together and made love.

A SMALL noise woke Mike. The fire had burned out, but there was enough moonlight to see a shadowy movement at the mouth of the smaller canyon. His heart began to beat very quickly, and he almost woke Goran up—but then he stopped. He couldn't disturb his lover at every little bump in the night.

At least it was very unlikely to be outlaws, he decided. Bandits would hardly be able to make a living off the few travelers who visited this shrine. Maybe it was a bundabeast. Were they seminocturnal?

"Miiiiichaellll...." The voice was hardly more than the whispering wind, and it made the hairs on his neck stand up. Another movement was just barely visible from the corner of his eye.

Dammit, grow a pair! he told himself angrily. He would go investigate. But he wasn't an idiot—he'd stay within earshot of Goran. He already knew how fast Goran could move when he wanted to.

Mike was already dressed. After he and Goran had sex, he'd put his clothes and boots back on against the night chill. Now he only had to extricate himself carefully from Goran's sleeping embrace and he could creep to the mouth of the side canyon.

"Miiiichaelll." The voice was a little louder now, a little closer. Taking a deep breath for courage, Mike stepped into the narrow space between the sheer rock walls. His boots splashed through the small stream, but he didn't care; they were waterproof. Very little light made its way into this crevasse. Mike kept one hand on a wall for balance and hoped it would keep him from tripping and falling on his healing face.

Something dark materialized directly in front of him. If he hadn't been immobilized with shock, he would have fallen on his ass.

"Michael," said the figure. And then it began to glow slightly from within, as if a few LED lights had been implanted in its skin. The glow cast just enough light for Mike to make out its face.

"Agata!" he exclaimed.

"Shh! Don't wake up that man of yours." She smiled slyly. "He's quite a man, isn't he?"

"I… what… what do you want? Ma'am," he added hastily, because it couldn't hurt to be polite.

"I wanted to tell you how pleased I am with you. A little praise always works well with humans. I didn't expect you to come this far."

He blinked at her. "You didn't?"

She twitched one shoulder. "I understand this was quite a shock to you. And I mistook your nature at first. Lord Meliach is a weak man. I expected you to be as well. But you aren't."

"Um, thank you."

This time, she gave him a regal nod. "Soon you will finish your task. My sister will be so put out!" She cackled like a naughty schoolgirl.

"And afterward…."

"I warned you. Do not ask a favor of me."

"Fine." He wasn't even sure what he'd ask her for at this point. Beg her to send him home, or beg her to let him stay? "But… it's getting really hard not to tell Goran where I'm from. I haven't though! He has no idea I'm from another world. And it's not fair. He told me all his secrets, and I have to keep this from him."

"You love him, don't you?"

"I care a great deal about him."

"Yes." She reached out and stroked Mike's uninjured cheek very lightly. Her touch was as hot as fire.

He gasped and his cock instantly hardened. "I don't—"

"Oh, I know. Don't like girls. Do you fancy me better like this?" Her face and body shimmered and changed, and now a very handsome older man stood before Mike, still glowing. The man had short gray hair and a square chin. He was built powerfully and wore tight leathers. He shimmered again and changed back to a middle-aged woman.

"H-how…?" Mike stammered.

"I am a god. It's a simple trick. This body and this face are of my own construction. I can appear in many forms. And all of them will make you hard and aching, Michael, for that is part of my power." She smiled. "Lust. It's an easy thing. But you have more with your man, haven't you? I can tell. Your heart beats with his."

Mike shook his head sharply. "I told you, I care for him. But I can't do more than that. I'm not capable of more."

She waved a dismissive hand. "That is preposterous. You've known him only a short time and yet already he is etched upon your soul."

"I don't believe in true love!" That came out louder than he'd intended. He looked nervously behind him.

Agata grasped his chin and turned his face toward hers. "True love, fate—whether you believe in them is immaterial. What matters is whether they believe in you. I told you this." She laughed softly and dropped her hand. "Go back to your man now, and keep your secret. Your pilgrimage will be completed very soon. And what happens before and after that, well, only my sister Ariana knows. She is the Weaver."

Without even a puff of smoke, Agata disappeared.

"More sisters? Fantastic," Mike grumbled as he turned to make his way back to Goran.

Chapter 16

THE FINAL shrine was near a town called Tesriya. Neither Mike nor Goran were unhappy that Tesriya was over a week's walk from Obrov. Both were glad for the excuse to spend a little more time together. But something was troubling Goran—something more than their upcoming separation—and as they cuddled together in a hayloft three days from Obrov, Mike finally brought it up.

"What's worrying you, big guy?" He was playing with Goran's chest hair, combing it this way and that with his fingertips and occasionally giving it little tweaks.

"We're heading west."

"Is that a problem?"

"We're going to pass very close to where I lived as a child."

Mike stilled his hand. "Is that dangerous? Will someone recognize you?"

"I don't know." Goran didn't sound especially concerned about this possibility.

But Mike was worried about it. "What if they realize you killed the lord? Won't you want to—"

"Nobody will care. After his death, his heirs fought each other viciously—so much so that they got distracted and other lords were able to come back in and snatch up the lands he'd stolen. There's nobody who cares to avenge him."

Well, that was good. But then what was the problem? Mike had learned by now not to push. He remained quiet, gently stroking Goran's chest.

Eventually, Goran sighed. "I'm sorry. I'm being foolish."

"I doubt that."

"I haven't been back there since my father died. I don't know if I can.... It haunts me." He gave a sad sort of laugh. "I'm plagued by far too many ghosts."

"Would it help to see it again? With a friend at your side?"

Goran's breath hitched slightly. "I don't.... It would add an extra day to our journey."

"So? I'd be happy for more time with you. And if a detour pisses Alina off, well, screw her."

Goran gave him a fierce hug, squeezing him so tightly Mike could barely breathe. "Thank you," Goran said and planted a kiss atop Mike's head.

Two days later—after a night of especially vigorous and intense sex—they turned onto a small road leading through a thick forest. Goran held himself stiffly as he walked, but he relaxed a little whenever Mike bumped against him or fondly squeezed his ass. This forest was thicker than the ones Mike had seen before, the path more overgrown. At times the trail disappeared completely and Mike would have worried they were lost, except Goran was obviously confident about the way.

"Nobody has hunted here for a long time," he said at one point as a deer nonchalantly strolled in front of them.

"Do you think you were the last one? You and Pavo?"

"Maybe. Or maybe the lord had men here until he died. I don't know."

Their footfalls were barely audible on the leaf-blanketed ground, and sunlight shone weakly through the boughs, giving the travelers the sense that they were deep underwater. It was easy to imagine they were the last two men in the world. And then Mike wondered if there *were* worlds like that, where only two men were left, and they loved each other but couldn't possibly procreate. That thought made him sad, and then he laughed at himself. To think that a short time ago, he didn't even believe in other worlds!

Goran was uncharacteristically quiet and Mike didn't want to disturb him, so instead he imagined all the permutations of himself that might exist. A world where he had been a better ballplayer, good enough to make the pros. One where he was straight, and one where he aced his English classes and sucked at math. A world where Benny never tore his heart out. No, aside from the ballplayer part, he liked his own life better. Benny was an asshole, and Mike was belatedly happy to be rid of him.

Mike was so lost in his musing that he didn't notice Goran had stopped until he'd almost walked into him. Goran made a soft noise as he stared ahead.

Ruins. Broken chunks of stone that looked to have been damaged centuries ago instead of decades. Tall trees grew through the rubble. One of the few intact portions of the castle wall surrounded a gaping hole where the main gate had once been. Whatever had once blocked the castle from invaders—unsuccessfully—was long gone.

But Goran's attention wasn't on the castle ruins themselves but rather on a small spot slightly off to the side. He moved a little closer with Mike in his wake, and Mike saw the foundation of what had once been a stone-and-wood building. A few of the charred timbers were still evident. Goran stopped again. "He's not here. Father. I… I almost expected to see his corpse. His skeleton."

Mike wasn't sure whether Goran was relieved or disappointed. "I don't see any signs of, um, bodies."

"Somebody must have buried them. There used to be a village nearby. Maybe they came."

"Do you want… do you want to build something? A memorial of some kind? I'll help."

"No." Goran shook his head. "Nobody would ever see it but me, and I already remember."

"I can remember too."

Goran gave him a brief but true smile and then a rough one-armed embrace. "Thank you."

"Gor? Tell me a happy memory of your family." Because that was what had sustained Mike after his father died—remembering all the good times. And there had been a lot of them. Those awful final months with the tubes and monitors faded in importance the more he recalled backyard ball games, happy celebrations, wonderful vacations. It mattered less that Dad had died weak and in pain when Mike thought about the time his father had come home from work early, filled a bunch of water balloons, and pelted Mike and Marie when they came home from school. Even Mom had joined in the ensuing melee.

"I was very small," Goran said quietly. "Five or six. Some of the older children had told me stories about a monster who crept into houses at night and ate small children. They said they were safe because they lived inside the castle walls, but not me. I was scared to sleep at night. And I guess those children knew that, because every day they had more terrible stories.

"I'm not sure how my parents found out. Maybe Pavo told them, although I told him not to. I didn't want them to think I was a coward. But they *did* find out, and every night for a week, my parents stayed awake by my side—my mother with her sword near at hand and my father with his bow.

"And one night my father said he heard a noise outside the hut. 'Stay inside!' he told me. 'You'll be safe here with Mama.' I knew Papa could beat any monster, so I wasn't afraid for him. He went out into the night. A few minutes later there was shouting and a terrible howling. And then Papa came rushing back inside. 'Come see!' he bellowed.

"Mama and I ran outside. Right on our doorstep was this… creature. It was horrible. Teeth, claws…. But it was dead. Papa had killed it."

Mike couldn't help interrupting. "What was it?"

Goran laughed softly. "Nothing real. I didn't realize it until years later, but Mama and Papa had patched together the most frightening parts of several creatures to create a monster. At the time I thought it was real. And even better, that very night Papa dragged the corpse into the castle—he must have planned this ahead of time with the night guards—and to the room where some of my worst tormentors lived. I got to come along. He pounded on the door. Those children's parents must also have been in on it, because they just opened the door and stood back. As soon as the children came to see, Papa held up his monster and *roared*! Two of the boys actually pissed themselves, they were so scared.

"And Papa said, 'Look what Goran and I killed!' He sounded so sure of himself that I think I began to believe I really *had* helped. Every child in the castle certainly did, even Pavo. I was a hero after that."

Tears were coursing down Goran's cheeks, but he was smiling. Mike folded him into an embrace. "Your parents loved you so much, Gor."

"I know."

"They'd be proud to see you now."

Goran buried his face in the crook of Mike's neck. "Why? I'm nothing."

"You're brave and strong and kind and loyal and loving. You're smart and you're sweet. You're the best man I know."

Goran snuffled, but Mike thought he felt a smile against his skin as well. "Don't forget handsome and a good lover," Goran said.

"As if I could forget that."

With a noisy sigh, Goran pulled away. He gave Mike an apologetic grin before moving off a few yards. He stood beside his old home, head bowed, murmuring quietly. Mike waited. He watched as Goran knelt, unsheathed his knife, and laid it on the ground. Then he stood and rejoined Mike.

"Were you making an offering?" Mike asked.

"Yes. To Lovacha. She's the god of hunters. My parents always honored her."

"But your dagger...."

"I can buy another when we get to Tesriya. You're not the only one who must make sacrifices."

Goran was still slightly subdued as they headed back to the main road, but a good deal of his original sparkle had returned to his eyes. He even sang a little, although the tunes were on the mournful side.

"GOR?" MIKE began hesitantly a couple of hours later. "What happens to people when they die?"

"You're asking me? You're the man who met a god."

"The subject didn't come up."

Goran climbed over a large fallen log. Mike chose to go around, which meant he had to hurry to catch up. When he did, Goran slung an arm around him. "My mama always said it didn't matter—everyone would find that out soon enough. Concentrate on a good life, she said. The priests say that if we're good, we go to serve the gods forever. Which doesn't really appeal to me all that much, actually."

"Me either." Mike was serving gods enough as it was.

"I like to think about Goran the Hunter, up in the sky. Maybe when we die, we get to visit the stars."

Christ. Mike was so close to spilling his secret he had to bite his tongue. "I like that idea," he managed to say.

"Maybe... I know you have to return to California. But maybe someday we'll meet again, up there." Goran pointed upward.

Hell. Maybe someday they would.

Chapter 17

THE ROAD to Tesriya wasn't nearly long enough for two wanderers who didn't want the journey to end. Mike and Goran were dragging their feet by the time they neared their destination. They entered through the main gate in the late afternoon, and a pair of bored guards and a few equally bored townspeople watched them pass without comment.

"The shrine is about a league from here," Goran said. "At the top of that hill." He pointed to a green mound that rose some distance from the town walls.

"I would hate to walk back downhill in the dark. Maybe we should wait until tomorrow."

Goran grinned. "Good plan."

Tesriya was a small town. Not desperately poor like some of the places Mike had seen near the beginning of his pilgrimage, but a little shabby. It was clearly a backwater, one of those places where nothing much ever happened and that few people outside the region ever thought about. The locals were dressed very plainly, and the shops were few and sold only the most utilitarian wares.

"This is the kind of place where people wore mullets and parachute pants even in 2004," Mike said.

"What?"

"Never mind."

They found a shop that sold instruments of destruction: knives, swords, spears, and a variety of other sharp things Mike couldn't identify. While Mike tried not to die of boredom, Goran spent an eternity trying out every knife in the place. It reminded Mike of when he was small and Marie and his mother dragged him to the shoe store. Even once Goran found a blade that satisfied him, he engaged in a long and spirited round of haggling with the shopkeeper. All of this apparently constituted the best entertainment available, because a small crowd filled the shop, watching and chiming in. In that respect, Mike decided, this was more like one of his father's hardware-store forays. Every man in the store always seemed to have an opinion about each other's home improvement projects: *Nah, you don't want a slotted hex washer on that one. Use a Torx pan head instead.*

When the locals weren't butting into Goran's business, they were giving Mike very strange looks. Maybe they didn't understand why he wasn't having fun too. He ignored them.

Mike was relieved when Goran finally completed the purchase and sheathed his new knife. "Dinner?" Goran asked as they walked out onto the street. "I have enough coppers left for an inn tonight."

"Sounds good." No point in arguing on what was likely to be their last night together.

There wasn't much choice of accommodations—Tesriya boasted a grand total of two inns. They chose the one that looked slightly less likely to house rodents in the kitchen. Besides, that one had a bigger common area, which meant the smoke from the fire and the stink of sour ale and unwashed bodies was less oppressive. The place was crowded, and everyone turned to stare until Goran glared at them. Mike and Goran found an empty table near the door, and Mike sat while Goran negotiated with the landlord. Goran must have been successful, because he returned to the table with two tankards and a wide grin. "Food'll be out shortly. And he says he has a private room. He claims he'll find better linens for us. Don't know what he means."

"I bet it's not as nice as the White Hart."

Goran lightly punched Mike's arm. "I've spoiled you."

Mike's answering smile was a little strained. Goran *had* spoiled him. Mike would never meet someone like him again.

They sat and sipped their ale, watery though it was. Mike's stomach grumbled loudly enough that Goran heard it and laughed. "I guess I haven't been spoiling you enough if you're starving."

"Maybe not. But I saw you eyeing that guy's stew—or whatever he's eating."

"Hmm. I bet we could polish off a good chunk of bundabeast tonight, if we had one."

"Bundabeast. It's what's for dinner."

Goran tilted his head. "Sometimes you say the strangest things. I wonder—"

"My master wishes to speak with you."

Mike looked up sharply at the same time as Goran jumped to his feet, his hand on the hilt of his sword. The man who'd spoken was dressed in fancier clothing than anybody else they'd seen. He was accompanied by two armed men. Mike put his hand up to halt Goran and the entire inn went silent, just like in a bad movie when the gunslinger enters a bar. This particular man looked a little old and chubby to be a good fighter, but his pals were in pretty good shape.

"Who are you?" Mike demanded.

The man gave him an extremely disdainful look. "I am the private secretary of the Right Honorable Lord Meliach. His lordship wishes to speak with you. Now."

Oh, shit. "He's here in Tesriya?" Mike shot Goran an uneasy look.

"Of course. And he is quite impatient."

Mike's mind veered crazily to Florence Richardson—the secretary to the CFO of Mike's company—a whip-thin woman who terrorized the entire finance department and could emasculate her boss with a single glance. But even Ms. Richardson didn't show up at a cubicle flanked by men with swords.

Mike stood. "Fine. I'll go." He turned to Goran. "Wait for me here. Keep my dinner warm, okay?"

"You are not going anywhere without me."

"But I have to talk to Lord Meliach and… and you're not… not supposed to—"

"You are *not* going anywhere without me." Goran crossed his arms over his chest.

"But Agata told me I can't—"

"*Not.*"

The entire room was staring at them—they had evidently topped the knife-shopping experience—and the secretary was looking increasingly pissed off. Agata was just going to have to deal, Mike decided. This was out of his hands. It was fate, maybe.

Mike nodded. He stood and trailed Meliach's men out of the inn. Goran followed so closely he was nearly stepping on Mike's heels.

They made their way down the cobbles like a strange and well-armed parade. Fortunately, the parade route was brief. The secretary stopped at one of the town's fancier houses and knocked sharply. As soon as the door opened, he led them inside.

They went up a set of creaky wooden stairs, down a hall, and into a large room. Two men sat in carved wooden chairs on either side of a large fireplace. One of them was the blond man who'd mistaken Mike for Meliach when they were in Varesh. And the second one—

"Good gods!" Goran exclaimed.

Lord Meliach rose from his chair, stalked across the room, and stopped inches in front of Mike. It was very disconcerting—like looking into a mirror where the reflection didn't quite match. Meliach was exactly Mike's height and probably within a few pounds of his weight. His cowlick was standing up, as it tended to do late in the day, and his canine teeth were long and sharp. Mike wondered if Meliach got called "vampire boy" when he was a kid too. His nose had the bump that Mike's mother always blamed on a baseball mishap but that his dad had whispered came through Mom. Meliach even had the freckle on one cheek that Marie used to teasingly call Mike's beauty mark.

They stared at each other.

Meliach's friend came over too. "He didn't have that wound on his face when I saw him before. That's why I thought—"

"Yes," Meliach interrupted, "I can see that it's a fresh scar. Who are you?" he asked, clearly questioning Mike.

"Michael Carlson."

Meliach chewed on this a moment. Then Blondie spoke up. "Is it possible you have a twin? Perhaps—"

"It is *not* possible. Besides, even among twins, have you ever seen such a close resemblance?"

Everyone in the room shook their head, including Mike. Marie's good friends Jenna and Janine were identical twins—the kind who dressed alike even as adults. It was easy to mistake one for the other. But if you saw them standing next to each other, there were clear differences.

"*What* are you?" Meliach asked. "And why are you on a pilgrimage to Alina's shrine?" He didn't look pleased. Mike very much hoped he never displayed that cold glint in his own eyes.

"Mike? What's going on?" Goran looked bewildered.

Mike's head hurt, and his brain couldn't come up with a single explanation that was likely to satisfy Meliach. Mike wasn't stupid, and probably Meliach wasn't either. They could sniff a load of bullshit from pretty far away. As a last-ditch effort, Mike attempted evasion. "I can't tell you. Look, I promise I'm no threat to you. I'm doing... something I was told. I'm almost done. Then I'll go back home and you can forget you ever saw me. I think... things in your town might improve after I go."

"Improve? How?"

Shit. "Things will be put right. People will die again."

Meliach narrowed his eyes. "Where are you from? Who are you? Who sent you?"

Mike wondered if that was what he acted like when payroll was late with their reports again. "I'm from California. That's really... far away. I was brought here by Agata."

Oh, Mike knew that expression: pissed-off disbelief. "You claim to be sent by a god? You?" Meliach added an extra sneer at the end.

"I... I can't.... Just let it drop, okay?"

Meliach marched to his secretary and whispered something in his ear. The secretary nodded and quickly left the room. Within seconds, running footsteps approached down the hall and eight more men burst into the room, each with a sword in hand. Goran growled and drew his own weapon.

"Kill him," Meliach said, pointing at Goran.

The guards stepped forward, and Goran dropped into a fighting stance. Mike yelled, "No! Don't you fucking hurt him!" Because he was pretty sure even Goran couldn't handle ten-to-one odds. He tried to dart between Goran and the guards, only to be pushed back by Goran. He almost stumbled into Meliach's arms.

The lord raised an imperious hand. "Wait," he said to his men. He looked expectantly at Mike. "Tell me or he dies."

"He has nothing to do with it! He's a guy I hired, that's all. He doesn't know any more about where I'm from than you do. Just let him go."

Goran shot him an angry look. Even if all the swordsmen miraculously stepped aside, there was no way he'd abandon Mike.

For a very long moment, nobody moved. It was Mike who broke the silence. "Fuck this. Fuck you, and fuck Agata and Alina and their whole fucking family." He sighed. "Get your goons to back off and I'll tell you everything."

Meliach gave a small nod. His guards put away their weapons, and all but two left the room. Mike was pretty sure the rest waited just outside the closed door. Goran reluctantly returned his sword to his hip but then walked over and stood very close to Mike. Everyone waited for Mike to talk, while he waited to see if the heavens would open up and rain down fire. Or maybe that wasn't Agata's gig. She was a sex god. Maybe if she got really mad, she made your junk shrivel and fall off.

"I'm from a place called California," Mike began. "I'm nobody special. Not a lord or anything. Um, we don't really have lords there anyway. I'm just a guy with an okay job and a decent apartment and a car that's almost paid off. And then one day Agata showed up. Yes, Agata the god. She just zapped herself into my apartment—*poof.*" He blushed slightly as he remembered what he'd been doing at the time.

"A god showed herself to you at your home?" Meliach asked coldly.

"Yep. I'd never heard of her. Because the thing of it is...." He took a deep breath. "I'm from another world."

"You're *what*?"

"From another world. It's… it has some things in common with this one. Like language. But there are differences too. And I didn't even believe in other worlds, okay? But Agata brought me here—just *boom*! First I'm there, and then I'm here—and after a while it's hard to keep denying things. She told me about you. Showed me your statue. And she told me how you'd made a promise to Alina when you went to that wedding celebration, but then you broke it."

Meliach's face went a disturbing shade of red. They didn't have high blood pressure, did they? Mike hadn't had a physical in a while.

"Nobody knows that," Meliach hissed.

"Alina sure does. And her sister too."

Goran's mouth was hanging open, and Meliach's friend looked pale and shocked. Even the secretary and the guards looked flabbergasted. "Another world, Mike?" Goran asked quietly.

Mike squeezed his arm. "I'm sorry. Agata said I wasn't allowed to tell anyone. Jesus, I wanted to tell you so badly! Now you know why… why we can't last. Why I can't take you back with me."

Mike wanted to cry, which was stupid. He didn't cry—apart from that little breakdown in the temple—and now was not the time. But Goran looked as if someone had torn out his heart and eaten it, and it was Mike who'd done that to him. Mike was a bigger asshole than Benny ever was.

"Why are you here?" Meliach snarled. His hands were clenched at his sides.

"You didn't keep your promise and Alina cursed your people. You know that, but you're too much of a selfish prick to care, aren't you? But Agata had this idea that if *I* did the pilgrimage gig in your place, it still might work. Because I'm you, in my world."

"That doesn't make any sense."

"No, but it's true. Look, I know all about you because you're me. You're lactose intolerant—too much dairy and you end up with belly cramps and a long date with your chamber pot. You can wiggle your little toes without moving the others. Rosemary gives you a rash—" He stopped. "You do have rosemary here, right?"

Meliach gave a cautious nod. "I don't allow it in food."

"Me either. Pain in the butt at Italian restaurants. When you were a kid, you wet the bed until you were way too old for it because—"

"I did not!" But Meliach was blushing—a dead giveaway and one that Mike could never control.

"You did, because our bladder developed slowly. We outgrew the whole problem before our teens, thank God. And I could go on. I can catalog our birthmarks and tell you exactly how long our cock is, soft and hard, and… do you know how to read?"

"Yes." The answer came from between gritted teeth.

"I bet you had trouble learning because we're mildly dyslexic. Um, we used to get the letters backwards, stuff like that. We're shitty spellers. But you've always been good with numbers."

Lord Meliach stalked to his chair. He picked up a bottle of wine from a small table, filled a goblet to the brim, and downed it. Then he refilled it and drank more. He closed his eyes for a very long time before opening them again. Maybe his head hurt too. Mike hoped so.

"I could have you killed right now," Meliach said.

Mike shivered, because he knew that was the truth. "I wouldn't recommend it. You're already on Alina's naughty list. You want to make Agata angry too?"

Meliach contemplated that. Maybe he shared Mike's speculations about detached dicks, because he shuddered. "What are your intentions?"

"Tomorrow I'm going to Alina's shrine and telling her we're really fucking sorry you're such a douche bag. And then Agata sends me home. Your subjects will start dying properly again, you can return to being Lord Ass Hat, and that's it. Story over."

"You don't intend to stay here?"

"I don't know how much choice I have in the matter, but no." Mike gave an anguished look to Goran, hoping his lover would understand. "My family's there. It's my home. It's where I belong."

Goran, his eyes still glazed with shock, couldn't respond.

After draining his cup for a second time, Lord Meliach came closer. "You have told nobody who you are?"

"No. I told you. Agata said not to."

"Not even the people of this town?"

"I don't think I've said a word to anybody but you and your secretary since we got here."

Meliach chewed his lip—one of Mike's nervous habits that he'd tried to break. Mike could tell when he reached a decision. "You cannot stay in this house. It belongs to the mayor. He nearly pissed himself with pleasure to be hosting nobility, but I can't have him see us together."

"What are you doing here, anyway?" Surely Meliach hadn't decided to apologize to Alina on his own.

"Edi told me of your encounter in Varesh." He waved vaguely at his friend, who was still gaping like a dying fish. "And he told me you were visiting Alina's shrines. I assumed you'd appear here eventually. I've been waiting for you for some time."

"Sorry to inconvenience you," Mike spat.

"Leave the town immediately. Make your offering in the morning. And then leave. If I see you again—"

"Not if I can help it." Mike hoped never to see Meliach's face again—except perhaps in the mirror.

After another pause, Meliach turned to his secretary. "Have four of my men accompany these two out of the town." To Mike he said, "If you create any problems—"

"The only one making problems here is you. We were about to sit down to a quiet dinner. You're the one doing all the strutting and sword-waving."

A particularly nasty smile appeared on Meliach's face. Mike sincerely hoped he never looked like that. "Are you prepared to make your offering at the shrine?" Meliach asked.

"I've made all the others." And then, because Meliach continued to sneer at him and because Mike really needed to know, Mike added, "What am I supposed to give her this time?"

"Oh, nothing important. You simply have to sacrifice something you love."

Shit, shit, shit. Okay, Mike would think about that later. Right now it took all his effort not to punch the smirk right off that familiar face. It wouldn't be a fair fight, considering Mike's right arm wasn't fully healed and Meliach had at least a dozen men on his side. Instead, Mike mirrored that sneer. "Now I know why you wouldn't do the pilgrimage. You don't love anyone but yourself."

Oh, that made the bastard angry! "You don't know me!"

"I know you as well as you know yourself. You're selfish and self-centered. You like to think you're very cool and logical, but the truth is you're just all caught up in yourself. Your heart is like ice. And not only will you never love anyone else, but you know what? Nobody is ever going to love *you*."

Meliach answered with a low growl. "Get out."

"Happily."

Mike grabbed Goran's arm and pulled him out of the room. He was right—the eight guards were waiting in the hallway. They looked as if they were trying to hide smiles. Maybe their boss wasn't all that popular among the troops.

Chapter 18

FOUR OF the guards followed Mike and Goran down the stairs and onto the street. None of them said a word as they walked. Mike felt very small leading five large men, and Christ, he was exhausted. But he kept his back straight and his steps firm. He stopped, however, when he came to a bakery, causing his entire entourage to skid to a halt. "We haven't eaten," Mike said to the guards. He was trying to channel a little of Meliach's imperial attitude; it came to him more easily than he expected. "Wait here while we buy some dinner."

He didn't know whether it was orders coming from their boss's look-alike that convinced the guards to obey, or pleasure that Meliach had been taken down a notch or two. Maybe they were just decent human beings who didn't want Mike and Goran to starve. In any case, one of the guards nodded slightly.

As Mike and Goran entered the shop, Goran leaned down to whisper in Mike's ear. "I gave my last coins to the innkeeper."

"Don't worry about it."

The boy behind the counter was in his early twenties and adorable, with spiky dark hair, huge eyes, and a sweet mouth. Looking slightly terrified, he gaped at Mike.

Mike pasted that sneer back on his face. "Do you know who I am, boy?"

"Of-of course, sir." The kid rendered a clumsy bow.

"Good. Give us a half dozen of those." Mike pointed at a pile of meat pies wrapped in flaky pastry that he'd become quite fond of in this universe. "You can send the bill."

"Yes, sir! Of course." The boy rushed to choose the biggest of the pies, which he placed reverently in a thin cloth sack. He held the bag out, but Goran grabbed it before Mike did. Good. Meliach was probably too high and mighty to carry his own dinner. "Th-thank you, sir!" the boy stammered.

Mike couldn't help himself—he dropped the kid a wink. "Have a good evening."

Back outside the bakery, Mike turned to the guard who'd earlier given him a nod. "When they send the bill to Lord Meliach, will you make sure it gets paid?"

The guard grinned. "It'll be my pleasure, sir."

Since Tesriya was small and the streets were mostly empty, it took barely ten minutes to reach the gate opposite where Mike and Goran had originally entered. This entrance was much narrower and was guarded by two sleepy-looking men in shabby uniforms. They must have recognized Mike—or misrecognized him, more accurately—because without a word, they scrambled to unbolt the door. Mike passed through with his chin held regally high and his retinue following.

The road on this side was a relatively narrow path, wide enough for only two men abreast. It was lit only by the last of the reflected twilight because there was just a sliver of moon. The path began to rise almost at once. The guards huffed and puffed. Apparently Meliach had lax exercise requirements for his men. Mike judged they were roughly halfway up the hill when they came to a flat spot, a sort of meadow covered in low grasses and flowers.

Mike stopped. "We'll sleep here tonight. You can go back and assure Lord Shithead that I won't return to Tesriya, and I won't step foot in Dalibor again."

"Very well," said the guard in charge. "I wish you well, sir." He and his men marched loudly away.

With a grunt of relief, Mike dropped the rucksack from his shoulders. He sat next to it, pleased that the ground was soft.

"Do you want me to find wood for a fire?" Goran asked softly.

"No, thanks. It's warm enough tonight, and we don't have to cook anything."

Goran sat opposite him and handed him one of the pies. It was very good. The filling was generous and nicely spiced. Mike and Goran each silently ate two, and they washed them down with swallows from Goran's water skin.

"Sorry I blew our chances of sleeping in a bed tonight," Mike said when the food was gone.

"I've slept in worse places than this."

"So have I."

They lay down next to each other, not quite touching, looking up at the sky. "Mike?" Goran said softly.

"Yeah?"

"Is… is California up there?"

"I don't know. Maybe. Our stars look different than yours."

Goran's noisy sigh interrupted the quiet night. "It must be very hard to be so far from home."

Mike's chest ached so fiercely it was hard to breathe. He missed his home desperately. But Christ, how could he face never seeing Goran again? He moved his arm over a bit to grasp Goran's hand. "I'm sorry, Gor. I should have told you, no matter what Agata said. This isn't fair to you."

"Wouldn't have mattered. I'd have fallen in love with you anyway."

"And I tried not to fall in love with you."

"But you do love me."

Mike squeezed Goran's hand. "I do love you." He rolled over so that he was wrapped in Goran's arm, his head resting on Goran's broad chest. "I had to go all the way to another world to find true love."

"If there's a version of you here, maybe there's a Goran in your world."

"He wouldn't be you. It's *you* I'm in love with, Gor, not someone with your face and body."

Once in a while when he wanted to kill time, Mike liked to play sudoku. Making those neat rows of numbers add up properly was very satisfying. But now Mike's life—and Goran's too—had become an unsolvable puzzle. Nothing added up, and all that remained was chaos and a vast looming chasm of loss.

But they had a few hours left together, at least, and the night was warm, the ground springy and fragrant. They undressed each other, their movements as slow and reverent as if it were their wedding night. In fact, that thought made Mike pause as he drew Goran's trousers off.

"Is something wrong, Mike?"

"How do you get married here? I mean, is there a ceremony?"

Goran's voice sounded tight. "You want to marry me?"

"I…. It's selfish, seeing as I'm probably leaving you tomorrow. But yeah, I do." He chuckled wryly. "Maybe one night of wedded bliss is as much as this commitment-phobe can handle."

"Why do you want to marry me?"

"Because… I don't know. So you know that I'm really serious about you. So that later I can think to myself, somewhere I have a husband I love. It's stupid. I'm sorry. It's not fair to you and—"

"Marry me!" Goran grabbed Mike's shoulders almost hard enough to hurt.

"Why?"

"Because then I'll know I have family, even if we're apart."

Fuck. Mike was crying again. He fought to keep his voice even, and he hoped Goran couldn't see his tears in the darkness. "What do we have to do?"

"Pavo and I went to a temple and pledged our love in front of a priest. It was very simple. But we don't have a priest here…."

"I think we can go one better than that. I think Agata's sort of keeping an eye on me. Can she officiate?"

Goran's laughter was loud and joyful. "Perfect." He scrambled to his feet, pulling Mike up alongside him. They were both naked. The slight breeze caressed Mike's body gently.

Standing very tall and straight, Goran spoke in a booming voice. "My Lady Agata. Please bear witness to my love for this man. I pledge him my heart, my loyalty, my protection, my soul. Please… please reunite us someday up there." He raised his hands to the sky. Then he dropped them, turned to Mike, and kissed him hard enough to steal Mike's breath away. "Your turn," he whispered.

"I have a hard-on," Mike whispered back. He wasn't sure why they were whispering.

"Me too. All the better! A fitting way to honor Agata."

Well, that was probably true. "Do I have to say the same thing?"

"Say what's in your heart."

Mike wasn't good at speeches. He thought for a moment. Then he spoke in his loudest, firmest voice. "My Lady Agata. You brought me here unwillingly. But now I'd like to thank you, because without you, I'd never have known this man. He's such a good man, Agata. Far more than I deserve. I promise to tell Mom and Marie about him so he can truly be a member of our family. I pledge him my heart, my loyalty, my protection, my soul. If there is a heaven in my world or his, I hope we can be together there."

He kissed Goran as thoroughly and ardently as he was able—which was pretty damn well.

At some point the kissing became more. They fell to the ground and moved against each other, seeking to become one in body as well as in spirit. Sometimes Mike was on top and sometimes Goran—it didn't matter, and most of the time Mike couldn't discern which way was up. It was as if the great, deep sky had swallowed them and they floated and tumbled in the star-speckled blackness. There was no yesterday and certainly no tomorrow, no worlds here nor there. Just the two of them and the universe and the sweet heat of their bodies together.

They came with ragged cries and lay tangled together, spent and complete.

"We may be having a very short honeymoon," Mike said when he could speak again, "but I wouldn't trade it for a month in Maui."

Goran chuckled and ruffled Mike's hair. "I even love you when you make no sense."

"I wish… now that you know my secret, I wish I had time to tell you about my world, Gor. It has a lot of problems. But there are such wonderful things too!"

"Like what?"

"Like… driving up Highway 1 in Mendocino, watching the Pacific Ocean crash on the rocks. Like smartphones. Like seeing the sunrise over the top of Yosemite Valley. Like… Thai food. Jumbo jets and swimming pools and antibiotics and a really good baseball game." He chuckled. "And sexy underwear and great footwear."

"I wish you had time to explain all that to me."

After a long period of sleepy silence, Goran kissed Mike's forehead. "Mike? Will you teach me a song from your world?"

"Ugh. You heard what an awful singer I am."

"I don't care. And there's nobody else to hear but me. Please?"

Mike rubbed his face. "What kind of song?"

"You could teach me the one you were singing when I first saw you."

"The national anthem? Good gods, no. How about…." He chewed his lip. "How about a song about California? One I'm going to mangle less horribly."

"Good. Perfect."

Mike took a deep breath. If there was a Don Henley god in this world, now would be a good time for that deity to help out. Mike opened his mouth and began to warble about a dark desert highway.

Chapter 19

MIKE NOW knew how it felt to wake up on the morning of your execution. It wasn't a good feeling, not even if your brand-new husband smiled at you and kissed you and sang "Hotel California." The sky was blue and innocent; birds trilled somewhere. There were delicious leftover pies to eat. It was a beautiful day. Mike was miserable.

It didn't take them long to perform their morning rituals and assemble their few belongings. They held hands as they began walking up the path, exactly as newlyweds should. Mike felt absurdly like Dorothy strolling the yellow brick road.

Something had been bothering him since the night before. Well, several somethings, but he chose to address only this one. "Gor? Are you going to be safe? Meliach's probably not happy that you know his secrets."

"I am not afraid of Lord Meliach."

"I know. I mean, you're an amazing fighter and everything, and I guess you can keep a low profile if you think he's nearby, but—"

"He won't harm me." Goran sounded so definite that Mike dropped the subject. He didn't have any right to tell Goran how to live his life, and Goran was too stubborn to listen anyway.

The last part of the hill was steep. They both walked slowly, not because of the exertion required but because they didn't want to reach their destination. But of course it inevitably happened, and the site was as bleak and desolate as Mike's mood.

The entire hilltop was bare of vegetation, as though someone had bathed the entire summit with Roundup. Not a single blade of grass survived, not a twig or petal or stem. No sign of any living thing, in fact, not even a bug. In the exact center of the emptiness was a long, low altar of rough stone. It reminded Mike of a piece of Stonehenge laid flat, held above the barren ground by smaller blocks of stone. As they moved closer, Mike saw the altar was badly stained; rust-brown splotches and black charred spots marred the pale-gray rock. It was terrifying.

Even worse was what lay around and under the altar stone. "Oh no," Mike whispered.

Goran squeezed his shoulders comfortingly.

Bones. Some were animals. Dogs. Horses. But many of them were human, both adults and—horrifyingly—children.

"Human sacrifice?" rasped Mike.

"The offering has to be loved. You like your boots, Mike, and that underwear you left in Obrov, but you don't love them."

"No. I don't. But to kill a *person*, Gor! In cold blood, not in self-defense or revenge or during a battle. And someone you know and love…. How could anyone do that?"

"Desperate people can. If it means winning a war. Or stopping a plague. Or making sure that people aren't denied the peace of death."

Ice filled Mike's veins. He knew what was about to happen, and it was like being in one of those terrible dreams where a monster chases you and you can't fucking move, legs stuck in goddamn glue or molasses, and it's coming nearer and nearer. Only this was no nighttime phantasm.

Goran unbuckled his belt. He removed the knife and set the belt and sword on the dirt. He placed the knife on the edge of the altar, very close to Mike. And then he climbed onto the rock and lay down as if it were a bed. His arms were at his side, his legs very slightly spread. He looked relaxed. He even smiled a little when he turned his head to look at Mike. "Slicing the throat is easiest. The blood will spurt, but you don't have to worry about missing on the first try. And it'll be fast. Just cut deep."

"I…. No." Mike wanted to shut his eyes and cover his ears like a small child. He wanted to vomit.

"You said you love me, Mike, and I know it's true. What else do you have to offer?"

"I can't! I won't."

"You have to." Goran's voice was very gentle. "It's all right. You'll bring Meliach's people what they need, and you'll return to your family. And I…. It won't hurt me much. Probably less than that cut on your arm. You've seen my scars—you know I'm no stranger to the wrong end of a knife."

"But… you'll *die*."

Goran shrugged, which looked strange in his relaxed position. "I'll die anyway. In a fight or at the end of a rope or from too much drink. I've been dying for *years*, Mike. This time with you… I finally lived again. It was beautiful. More than I dreamed of. I am at peace, my beloved." He looked like he meant it.

Mike, however, was as far from peace as it was possible to get. The ice inside him had melted only to be replaced by a buzzing, whirling maelstrom. A puzzle that had no solution. He couldn't murder Goran. Would not. But on the other hand, he couldn't—

Oh, yes he could.

Mike scrambled onto the altar near Goran's head. As Goran crooked his neck in alarm, trying to see what Mike was up to, Mike dropped to his knees. "Alina! I give you my home."

Goran sat up quickly. "No! Mike!" He tried to reach for Mike, but Mike pushed him as hard as he could. It wasn't enough to topple Goran off the stone. He was heavy. But it caught him off-balance, and he fell to his side.

Mike spoke very, very fast. "I give you my home I love it I love my home more than almost anything in any world I renounce my request to return home." Maybe that was enough, but Goran was unmoving, so Mike added more, this time a little more slowly. "I've given you blood and tears and… and underwear. Please forgive that asshole Lord Meliach and take back your curse. Please don't make those people suffer any longer. I'm sacrificing my chances of returning home. I don't have anything to stab or, or burn, nothing even symbolic. But I'm sacrificing my hopes of home. Please let that be enough."

Nothing happened. Mike wasn't sure what he'd been expecting anyway. A clap of thunder out of the blue sky? A burning bush on the barren ground? All he got was Goran looking furious.

"How could you do that!" Goran yelled. He jumped off the altar and paced angrily, waving his arms around. "How could you do that? Your family, Mike, and all those things you talked about. I can't give you a good life here. You know how I live. I own nothing but what you see, I'm not good at much of anything except killing, I can't read, I can't—"

Mike scrambled off the altar and planted himself in front of Goran. "I don't care. I don't give a flying fuck if we spend the rest of our days eating raw bundabeast and sleeping on gravel. I love you. I am not going to murder you, and I'm not going to leave you."

Goran glared at him for about five more seconds before melting and scooping him into a fierce embrace. "You shouldn't have done this," Goran said.

"I've been making safe and predictable choices my whole life. Time for a stupid, noble sacrifice. Especially when I know in my heart it's the right decision." He sniffed. "And you called me beloved. I've never been a beloved before, and I don't want to stop now."

They both laughed and cried a little at the same time, which gave Mike the hiccups. Then they sat side by side on the altar. Goran put his knife away. Mike swung his feet. It was a beautiful day, Mike thought. He knew he'd grieve his loss soon enough, but not right now. Now he felt more comfortable with himself than he ever had before. Now his heart was open.

"Where should we go?" Goran asked.

"You tell me. It's your world."

"We could... would you like to go to Strazha? It's not all that far from here. We could stay for a while. I could find some work."

Mike shrugged. "Sure. Do you think I could find something too? I'm not feeble, you know."

"I know," Goran said with a slightly lascivious grin. "And you can read, which is rare enough. That could be useful."

"Sure. Or we could return to that village on the river road. We don't have any money for the White Hart, but maybe the locals would hire you to scare off bandits. And I could—"

A female voice interrupted him. "You are a very clever human."

Mike and Goran leapt off the altar, Goran ready to draw his sword. A woman—middle-aged, quite thin, and beautiful—stood in front of them. Mike recognized her from the statue he'd seen in Kutina. "Alina?" he squawked.

She nodded regally. Goran gasped and fell to his knees, but Mike remained standing. He hadn't bowed to Agata, and he didn't intend to bow to her sister. He did drop his head a bit, mimicking the clumsy bow of the boy at the bakery. "Um, hello," he said.

"I was positive you were going to give me that man." She pointed at Goran. "You surprised me. That doesn't happen often."

He wasn't sure whether that was a good thing or bad. She didn't seem angry, but he wasn't particularly experienced in reading gods' moods. "I made the right decision," he said.

"Perhaps."

"Is it… is it enough? Will you lift the curse on Meliach's people?"

Now she looked stern. "I already have. *I* honor my obligations, even if trickery has been used."

Goran had been turning his head back and forth, following their conversation. Now he rose and stood slightly ahead of Mike. "It wasn't his idea, my lady. He wasn't given any choice."

"There is *always* a choice. My sister Ariana spins the strands of fate, but humans weave them together."

Mike and Goran exchanged bewildered looks. Mike was going to ask Alina for an explanation, but another figure appeared next to her. No poof or pop or zap. Just not there one moment and there the next.

"I see you've met Michael," Agata said. She was smiling the same way Marie used to when she tattled on Mike and he got in trouble. It was the grin of the triumphant sibling.

Alina didn't seem startled or put out by Agata's sudden appearance. "I've been watching him for weeks. You're very pleased with yourself, are you not?"

"I chose so wisely! His decision today—choosing to protect his husband—that was delightful."

Goran looked nervous. Mike couldn't blame him. Poor guy had never met even one god before, and here he was faced with two of them. Mike grabbed Goran's hand and dragged him back a little so they were side by side.

The gods didn't pay either human any attention. They squared off with one another. "You enjoyed your game this time, sister, but next time perhaps I will triumph," Alina said.

"Next time? Sister, I have no need to curse humans who break their promises to me, because none dare to do so."

"None do so because the creatures would rather fuck than die. But they all come to me in the end, don't they?"

"At the very end. I have them for decades first."

The gods looked furious by now—a truly terrifying sight. Mike and Goran backed up as far as they could, which wasn't much. The altar was behind them. Mike hoped the gods forgot all about them, but he didn't know how likely that was. They were yelling at each other now, each god boasting about her own powers and belittling her sister's. They looked about two seconds away from a celestial face-clawing.

"Daughters!"

Now everyone was shocked—Goran, Mike, Agata, and Alina. A man had appeared; he was older, tall, and broad. He wore a tunic, but his face reminded Mike of the male newscasters that used to be so prevalent on the networks, the ones who were chosen for their resonant voices and fatherly, authoritative looks. And an odd thing happened. Well, *another* odd thing happened. All of a sudden Agata and Alina appeared much younger. They still scowled at each other, but now they resembled chastised teenagers. "Hello, father," they mumbled in unison.

"Oh, holy heavens," Goran breathed. He looked as if he might faint. "T-Tomismoran?"

Tomismoran didn't even glance their way. He was too busy glaring at his daughters. "You have disturbed me again!"

Alina took a step forward. "But father, I had given a perfectly fair punishment to a lying human, and *she* butted in. It was none of her business at all! She dragged this man all the way from another world just to make fun of me." She pointed at Mike, who wished he were invisible.

"That's not true!" Agata exclaimed. "I was concerned about those poor people. She was making them suffer and—"

"I wasn't making them suffer! It was that stupid lord. If he'd only kept his promise—"

"Then smite him, not those innocent—"

"You don't care about those people! You only wanted—"

"*Enough*!" Tomismoran's roar shook the ground. All the gods kept their feet, but Mike and Goran fell and landed on their asses. They stayed there. Seemed safer.

"I am wearied of your eternal bickering," Tomismoran said. "You are old enough to have learned to get along by now. Why can't you be quiet and obedient, like your sister Ariana?"

The goddesses made matching sour faces. They looked one step away from sticking out their tongues. But they remained silent, which seemed to mollify their father a little. He huffed. "What's done is done. You *will* find common ground over this matter. Alina. Did this human properly complete his pilgrimage?"

"Yes, Father."

"He made all the appropriate offerings?"

"Yes, Father."

"And were they sincerely given?"

She thought for a moment before nodding. "Yes, Father. They were."

"And although he is human, and he is not exactly the man who wronged you, has he found favor in your eyes?"

Alina gave Mike a long, considering look. It took all his will not to squirm, and he was relieved when she turned back to her father. "He understands the importance of death. And he was surprisingly fierce when confronted by bandits. Yes, he has found favor."

Mike let out a long, whistling breath.

But Tomismoran wasn't finished. "Agata, has this man done all that you asked of him?"

"He has, Father." Apparently she was willing to forgive Mike telling people about his origins.

"Has he found favor in your eyes?"

Again that long look. Mike hoped never to face scrutiny from a god again. But finally Agata nodded. "He is an ardent lover. Even believing that he would return home today, last night he authentically pledged himself to his beloved. He chose love over home." Her eyes sparkled. "And he gave Alina an undergarment as an offering. Yes, he has found favor."

Tomismoran looked satisfied. "Good. Then I will hear no more from either of you on this matter." He crooked a finger at Mike. "Come here, human."

Mike's knees felt weak, but he rose and stepped closer. Goran stood too, but Mike gestured him to stay where he was. For once, Goran listened. Tomismoran gave Mike a faint smile, and for a moment—just a fraction of a second—he reminded Mike of his own father. "You have done well under difficult circumstances, human. I will send you home now."

"Oh!" Mike's heart raced. "But I sacrificed—"

"I know what you did. You gave up your hope of home. But that doesn't mean I can't send you anyway. You don't belong in this world."

"I.... Thank you, sir. I didn't expect—"

"I know."

Mike turned to look at Goran, who stood all alone near the altar. Then he faced Tomismoran again. "Please, sir. I don't mean to be ungrateful or disrespectful. But I don't want to leave Goran."

"I understand, son. Your husband is a good man. He was willing to give up his own life for your happiness."

"He was. It's just... I don't think I'll ever be happy without him."

Tomismoran set a hand on Mike's shoulder. It was a huge hand—bigger even than Goran's—and very heavy. But the touch somehow made Mike feel a little stronger. Maybe a tiny bit of godly power transferred the way heat does. "Son, human lives are so short and yet so complicated. You take my daughter Ariana's strands and you braid and twist them about you until you can't see your own patterns any longer. Go home. See what you weave."

Mike wanted desperately to argue, but he recognized the expression in the god's eyes—Mike's father had one very like it. It meant the matter was settled. "Can I say good-bye, sir? Please?"

"Yes. But only briefly. I have other matters to attend to."

Mike rushed to Goran. There were no words for this situation, so they hugged as hard as they could and kissed, and Mike inhaled his husband's scent for the last time. "I love you," Goran said. "So much."

"Me too. Please, please take care of yourself. Promise me."

Goran nodded against him.

"Michael," Tomismoran called.

Mike tore himself away. It hurt more than any of his knife wounds, but he walked back to the gathered gods. Alina and Agata smiled at him—sweet smiles without any irony to them. "Safe journeys, son," said Tomismoran.

Mike's stomach plunged and everything went black.

Chapter 20

"MIKEY! YOU look like the weekend chewed you up and spit you out. Tell me you're ready to work on the quarterlies."

Mike glanced at his boss and sighed. "I'm living for it, Dan."

Dan clapped him hard on the shoulder. "Fantastico. What the hell happened to your face?"

Automatically, Mike touched the bandage on his cheek. He didn't really need to cover it anymore—it had healed well—but he couldn't think how to explain a weeks-old scar appearing over three days. "Got into a fight," he said.

"*You*? Really? Wow, didn't know you were such a wild man on your off time. Jekyll/Hyde thing, huh?"

"Something like that. Dan, if you want me to get these reports finished, I need to get to work."

"Sure thing, Mikey-Mikey." With another hard shoulder clap, Dan marched away from Mike's cubicle.

The spreadsheets weren't any comfort this morning. Yes, the numbers were all there, nicely lined up, and the equations were as neat and tidy as always. But there was a ragged hole in Mike's chest. It hurt so much that sometimes he glanced down at his lap, almost expecting to see bloody chunks that had once been his heart. He'd felt this way since Saturday morning, when he'd opened his eyes and found himself lying on his living-room floor.

He'd known at once it hadn't been a hallucination or a drunken delusion. For one thing, his rucksack was squished painfully under his shoulders and he was wearing the clothing Agata had stolen for him in Dalibor, along with the boots from Varesh. For another, he could see the scars on his arms and feel the one on his cheek. But most important was the horrible pain of loss—a pain no dream could conjure.

He'd checked his iPhone, sitting where he'd left it on the coffee table, and wasn't terribly surprised to discover he'd been gone only one night. If gods could yank him from one world to another, surely they could handle time differentials with no problem. "Thank you, Tomismoran," he said, grateful that he wasn't unemployed, homeless, and presumed dead. He was especially glad his mother and sister hadn't needed to mourn his loss.

He took a long, wonderful bath and put on clean, soft clothing— including underwear. He checked his e-mail. He ordered pizza. He lay down in his queen-size pillow-topped bed. And he cried. He spent most of the weekend like that—eating, napping, crying. When he slept he dreamed of Goran's smell, his taste.

But he got up at six on Monday morning as he always did, and he went for a jog, running through overzealous lawn sprinklers and dodging the garbage cans placed at the curbs for emptying. Then he showered and dressed in khakis, button-down, tie, and loafers, and he drove himself to work. And now here he was, working on the fucking quarterly reports while the remains of his heart lay pulsing in his lap.

The day crawled by. He couldn't lose himself in his work as he used to, and he was wiped by the time he e-mailed the reports to Dan at seven o'clock. He ordered Chinese for dinner, vegged in front of the TV for a short while, and went to bed early. Maybe that was the solution—work himself to exhaustion and he wouldn't have the energy to think about Goran. He could just be numb. He was aware this wasn't much different from Goran's attempts to drink his ghosts away.

But there was still something he had to do, a promise he meant to keep. On Tuesday he sent a text to Mom and Marie: *Have sthing important to tell you. My place for dinner on Sat?*

Marie answered him right away: *We already know ur gay, Mikey. LOL. See you Sat @ 7.*

And Mom wasn't far behind her: *What's the matter honey? Everything ok?*

Tell you on Sat, he answered.

He'd never been the praying type, and he wasn't sure Goran's gods could hear him in this world. But every day that week, he sat in his living room and addressed Alina, Agata, Tomismoran, and any deity who would listen. "Please keep Goran safe and well. Please help him be happy."

MIKE WASN'T the world's greatest cook and it was too hot for the oven, so on Saturday he bought a rotisserie chicken and a few other items at the grocery store. He got a couple of bottles of wine too. Alcohol was going to be a good thing tonight. He made a big salad with spinach, arugula, chicken, and mandarin oranges, and he sliced up a loaf of french bread. He cleaned his apartment. It wasn't actually that messy, but he always cleaned before his mother came over.

And then he waited, alternately pacing and staring blankly at the TV.

He heard his mother's approach before she rang the bell—her heels click-clacked on the sidewalk outside. As soon as he opened the door and she saw his face, she gasped. He'd intentionally not worn a bandage today. "Darling! What did you do to yourself?" She reached up to trace the scar.

"Cut myself shaving."

"Michael! Were you in an accident?" She twisted around, probably to see if his car was in the lot.

"No, Mom. Come in. This is… part of what I need to talk to you about."

She entered the apartment and looked around suspiciously, as if she expected something to leap out at her. When nothing did, she dropped her purse on the coffee table. The bag was enormous, covered in jangling buckles and with charms hanging from the zippers. He always wondered how she avoided back problems from lugging that thing around.

He smiled at her and began to set the kitchen table for dinner.

"Can I help, Mikey?"

"Nope. Everything's under control. Um, you can pour yourself a glass of wine if you like."

"Wine and not beer? Is this an occasion?"

"Not exactly."

She wandered for a few moments, peering through his windows and at his bookshelf. "Next time I'm bringing you a plant. I'll make some cuttings. You need greenery around this place. It's good for your lungs."

"Thanks. That'd be nice."

The bell rang again and Mom let Marie inside. Marie immediately exclaimed over Mike's cheek too. "He won't tell me what happened to him," Mom said. "It's a big mystery."

"I'll tell you soon enough. Let's eat first, okay?"

They sat around the kitchen table and had one of their usual conversations. That meant that Mike mostly stayed quiet while Mom and Marie bickered happily over TV shows, potential vacation destinations, politics, and dating habits. Mike couldn't help but smile at the familiarity of it, the comfort he felt when Marie reached over to adjust Mom's hair and Mom yelled at her for playing with hair at the dinner table. He loved them. It would have broken his heart never to see them again and to know they would have grieved and wondered over his sudden disappearance. His heart was broken anyway, of course. Unsolvable puzzle.

"Mikey, honey, tell us what's wrong." It was Mom's turn to break the rules; she smoothed Mike's hair back. "You look so sad."

"Let me clean up first and then I'll spill."

They waited impatiently while he put away the leftovers and washed the dishes. To be honest, he took his time over it. He was nervous about the upcoming discussion. But eventually the kitchen was spick-and-span. He ducked into the bedroom and came back out with a pile of things: his clothing from the alternate world and other souvenirs. He set them down on the coffee table and sat between the women on the couch.

Marie poked at the boots. "Are you suddenly into cosplay or Ren faires or something? Is that what you wanted to tell us?"

"Do I really seem the type?"

"I dunno. Maybe you're having an early midlife crisis."

He smiled at her. "Not yet. Um... I have sort of a long story to tell you guys. It's going to sound really wild. But I promise it's not a joke and I'm not crazy or anything. So if you could maybe just listen to the whole damn thing before drowning me in disbelief, I'd really appreciate it."

His mother and sister exchanged alarmed looks. He wasn't usually much for speeches or wild tales. Until Agata had shown up, he'd lived such a boring, predictable, safe life that sometimes he'd been a little tempted to make something up just to seem slightly more interesting. But he hadn't possessed the creativity for that.

He cleared his throat. "Last Friday night I was, um, hanging out at home." He decided not to tell them exactly what he was doing. Even thinking about it was embarrassing. "And this lady showed up. By showed up, I mean actually popped into my living room without using a door or window—just *poof!*—because she's actually a god and she wanted to take me to another world where I was supposed to go on a pilgrimage to atone for my alternate self's asshattery." He took a great whooping breath and let it out in a whoosh.

Mom and Marie were speechless—pretty much a first for either of them. He took advantage of it and forged ahead. "And that's what she did. Her name's Agata, by the way, and she's kind of in a perpetual feud with her sister Alina. Who's also a god, of course. Agata zapped me to this other world wearing nothing but my underwear. She told me if I ever wanted to get home, I had to visit all these shrines. Also, I was going to save an entire community who'd been cursed by Alina. I didn't really have any choice, so I agreed. It took me weeks and weeks, even though less than a day had passed when I returned here. And while I was there, I... I fell in love with a man named Goran, and I married him." He paused to let that sink in.

One of the things he dearly loved about his mother was her ability to remain levelheaded and bossy even under extreme circumstances. If the zombie apocalypse happened, she would stand calmly in the middle of the street, telling the neighbors where to seek shelter and how to fashion weapons. She didn't fail Mike now. She gave him a stern look and patted his knee. "Michael. You are going to explain what you're talking about. You're going to do it slowly and carefully and I am going to ask questions and you will answer them. But first you're going to fetch me another glass of wine. In fact, bring the whole bottle."

Impulsively, he gave her a quick hug. "Okay, Mom." And he followed her instructions—as he usually did.

Although Mom and Marie did ask quite a few questions as he talked on and on, neither of them dialed the loony bin to come cart him away. When he got to the part where he and Goran married, Mom and Marie got all misty-eyed. But then he got to the end—the part where he left Goran—and Mike suddenly broke down in huge, mortifying sobs.

Marie and Mom enveloped him in a group hug. After a while, Mom pulled a package of tissues from her purse and handed them over. "Sorry," he sniffed when he could speak again. "I gave Alina my tears in Varesh and now I can't seem to stop."

"It's okay, Mikey. It's good for you. Keeping all that emotion inside is bad for your stomach." She kissed his cheek.

He drooped against her and leaned his head on her shoulder. He hadn't done that in a long time, but he felt so goddamn drained. Didn't matter how old he was—sometimes a guy just needed his mother. He liked it when she started playing with his hair.

"So have you two decided I'm certifiable?" he asked.

Marie shook her head. "You're the sanest person I know."

"And frankly," his mother chimed in, "I don't think you have the imagination to make up a story like that."

"Gee, thanks," he said, but he was relieved.

His sister picked up the vest Agata stole for him and inspected the embroidery. "Besides, you have proof. This stuff, plus your scars. I just saw you... what? Two weeks ago? And you weren't sliced and diced then."

He sat up straight and looked back and forth between them. "So you're actually willing to believe this happened to me?"

"Maybe," Mom said. "Strange things happen. Remember when Uncle Edwin said he was abducted by aliens?"

"Uncle Edwin was a drunk, Mom."

"I know that. But after that, what happened? He never touched another drop of alcohol in his life. Sober as a judge until the day he died. None of us ever would have thought that was possible. And my friend Nina. She was diagnosed with cancer, and the doctors gave her only six to eight weeks. She refused chemo—didn't want to spend her last days like that, she said. But she was still alive three months later, and when she went to the doctor, they found no sign at all of the tumors. They were just gone. That was ten years ago, Mikey, and I just had lunch with her last week. Or our old neighbor, Camille. Remember her? Tiny little thing. One day she was walking with her youngest— What was that boy's name?"

"Derek," answered Mike. He'd had a crush on Derek when they were in their teens.

"That's right. Nice boy. Well, he was a baby in a stroller, and they were crossing the street. A car came speeding right at them! Camille tried to get away, but the stroller ended up caught under the car. And you know what she did? That tiny little thing *lifted* that car with her bare hands, all by herself, and kicked the stroller free. Poor Derek was a little bruised and scraped, but that was all."

"I remember that!" Marie exclaimed. "It was on the news and everything."

Mom nodded. "Mikey, the universe is much more amazing than you've ever given it credit for." She kissed his cheek again. "If you want to know the truth, the part I'm finding hardest to buy is that you finally decided to get married. I thought I'd be long in my grave before either of my children decided to settle down. And as for grandchildren...."

"Mom!" Marie and Mike cried in unison.

She grinned for a moment before her expression turned serious. "You really fell for this Goran, didn't you, honey?"

"Mom, I love him so much." His voice broke, but at least he managed not to start crying again. "I'd do anything to have him back."

"Actually, that will not be necessary."

You'd think Mike would be used to beings popping in and out by now, but he wasn't. And of course it was a first for Mom and Marie. Marie shrieked. Mom leapt to her feet, looking fierce. And Mike jumped about three feet straight up.

But when he saw who one of those beings was....

"Goran!" Mike yelled. He launched himself over the coffee table and into his husband's big, strong arms. Goran squeezed him fiercely and snuffled at the crook of Mike's neck.

They remained like that for a long time. Mike had nearly forgotten anyone else was in the room. But someone cleared her throat quite pointedly, and Mike and Goran separated a little. Not much— neither wanted to lose contact with the other.

"Hello," said an unfamiliar woman. Except she wasn't entirely unfamiliar. She wore a complicated outfit made of layers of knitted and woven shapes, and she bore a distinct resemblance to Agata and Alina. She looked younger, however. Closer to his age.

"Ariana?" Mike guessed.

She dimpled at him. "Of course. It's lovely to meet you, Michael."

"Uh, likewise. And… and this is my mom and my sister. Mom, Marie, this is Ariana. The god. I told you about her."

When Mike and Marie were little, they used to catalog and name their parents' expressions. Now Mom brought out her Company Smile. "I'm honored," she said.

That earned her a pleased nod from Ariana. Marie could only manage a sort of wave, but Ariana must have been used to people taken aback by her sudden appearance. She waved back.

The introductions over, Mike and Goran moved back into an embrace. Mike couldn't get enough of feeling that body against his, so solid and real. "How?" he asked. "How are you here?"

"My Lady Ariana, of course."

"But I don't—"

Ariana interrupted. "He made a pilgrimage to my shrine."

That made Mike pull away slightly to blink at his husband. "You did?"

"Yeah. It wasn't…. Gods, Mike, I've missed you so much! But then I got to thinking how lucky I was that our paths crossed, even if it was for so short a time. And I figured Agata got what she wanted already, by tricking Alina. And Alina got all those offerings from you. Even Tomismoran—you thanked him, and after you left, I thanked him too. But Ariana must have played a part in the whole thing, and nobody had thanked her. So I did."

Ariana smiled warmly. "People often curse me. Or they forget me or deny I exist. It's rare for someone to thank me for my work. Very rare. And Goran was so very sincere about it. He made me a very generous offering."

Mike frowned for a moment, trying to think what that might have been. But then it dawned on him what was missing. "Your sword!" he exclaimed. "You gave her your sword!"

"Yes." Goran shrugged. "Because it was important to me, and I wanted her to know how grateful I was. Besides, I'm tired of killing, Mike. I've had enough."

Mike kissed him—lightly, on the lips—just to let Goran know he was loved.

Ariana grinned mischievously. "Goran's gift touched me. But also I heard what my father said when Agata and Alina were squabbling again. 'Why can't you be more like Ariana?' Good, sweet, perfect, obedient Ariana. Well, I'm not so good and obedient, not always. I have a mind too! And since I was pleased with Goran anyway, I thought, why not send him here, if that's what he'd like? He's not supposed to be here, and my father and sisters will likely be quite put out." Her grin increased three notches.

"But... can he stay? If Tomismoran is angry—"

"I made a pledge to Goran that he may remain. A god's pledge is sacred. Nobody can break it—not even my father. Don't worry, Michael. Goran will stay with you forever."

Oh, gods. There were no words for what Mike was feeling. He supposed it was what a condemned man might feel if, on the eve of his execution, he were informed he'd been pardoned.

"Thank you so much," he said to Ariana. "If there's something I can give you to show how grateful I am—"

"Weave a beautiful life together. That will be thanks enough."

And she was gone.

That left the four humans in Mike's living room. Goran looked huge and oddly misplaced, with the TV behind him and his boots tracking Nenahde dust onto Mike's beige carpet. And although Goran was still clutching one of Mike's arms, he was frowning. Mike had a terrible thought. "Gor? Did you *want* to come here? It's not your world. It's going to be so different for you."

"I'd live on the moon if you were there, Mike."

"Then... Jesus, Goran. Welcome home." More hugs were in order, and they would have soon progressed to something more active, but Mom and Marie were watching. Mike looked at them a little self-consciously. "Mom, Marie... I'd like you to meet my husband."

They stared at each other. Mike would have been willing to bet Goran had looked less terrified going into battle. But then Mom flew around the coffee table, flung herself at Goran, and wrapped him in her arms.

"Welcome to the family, honey," she said.

Chapter 21

GORAN LEANED over the stone wall, a brisk wind whipping his long hair. "What are those, Mike?" He pointed far out and down, where a sandy peninsula jutted into the Pacific. The sand was dotted with brown shapes that looked big even this far away.

"Seals," Mike answered.

"Are they edible?"

"Um, I think so. But the State of California frowns on it. You'd probably end up in prison." Mike was slightly relieved Goran no longer carried a sword. Goran wanted to buy a new one to replace the one he gave Ariana, and Mike spent weeks patiently explaining why Goran couldn't walk around looking like he was ready to decapitate people. They'd ended up with a compromise: a big knife that Goran kept hidden inside his black motorcycle boots. The boots had sealed the deal. Goran had fallen in love with modern footwear, and with tight jeans and jockstraps.

"Oh," Goran said, slightly disappointed.

"Hey, you're the one who nixed the hunting trip."

Mike had a plan. He and Goran would rent a cabin and Goran could go after deer or turkeys or something. Mike even offered to do research on hunting regulations. But Goran had opted for the coast instead; he'd seen photos of the ocean and wanted to see it in person. Fine with Mike. Before Mike could make reservations, though, Goran used his newly developed phone skills and invited Mom, Marie, Jeff, and Cleve along.

"I thought we'd have a romantic weekend, just us two," Mike had said.

Goran gave him a quick hug. "We have lots of time together. I thought some family would be fun."

And he was right—family would be fun. Besides, Jeff had booked them condos owned by the timeshare company he worked for, which meant the lodging was free. And this way Mike would have a little audience for his planned surprise.

With the blue sky behind him and the blue ocean beneath him, with his hair a mess and his plain white T-shirt stretched over taut muscles, Goran was breathtakingly beautiful. Best of all was his smile. He looked like a man who'd permanently escaped his ghosts. "Will we be able to swim in the ocean?" he asked.

"You can give it a try. But it's really cold."

"I want to try anyway. But right now, I feel like I'm flying."

"We can someday, if you like. Go in an airplane, I mean."

Goran whooped like a child on Christmas.

They bundled themselves back into the car. Goran watched carefully as Mike started the engine, backed out of the space, and pulled onto the highway. Goran was looking forward to driving lessons soon, once his reading improved a little more and the lawyer they'd hired got his paperwork settled. The lawyer hadn't asked too many questions about why Goran had no ID. Maybe she thought Goran was an illegal alien—which was true, actually. But she was a friend of Marie's and good at her job, and she'd pulled a few acts of creative paperwork that Mike didn't want to know about. Soon Goran Carlson would have papers officially declaring him a citizen of the United States.

Mike's Civic hugged the curves as they twisted and turned their way north. The windows were rolled down so they could smell the salt air, and Goran sang along with Mike's MP3 player. He had a particular fondness for early eighties pop music, but Mike had banned any Olivia Newton-John in his presence. He ended up with a lot of Michael Jackson and Duran Duran instead. It was one of the hardships Mike now had to bear, along with the fact that his husband thought baseball was boring.

Goran drummed his fingers on the windowsill, and Mike smiled so broadly his face hurt. He'd been doing that a lot these past few months.

The other members of their party probably hadn't stopped at every scenic overlook along the way, so Mike and Goran were the last to arrive. Everyone exchanged hugs. If Goran wondered why Mom's embrace was especially enthusiastic, he didn't ask. They had three separate condo units, side by side, but the living rooms were a little cramped for six people. At Jeff's suggestion, they all walked down a sandy pathway that led to a boardwalk. After a few hundred yards, the boardwalk widened into a semicircle of several wooden benches with an ocean vista behind. Birds flitted back and forth through the brush, and gulls called from high overhead.

Everyone took a seat on the benches. Jeff and Cleve were practically in each other's laps, Mom and Marie weren't bickering for a change, and Goran looked radiant. He told Mike that sometimes he woke up in the morning afraid it had all been a wonderful dream. Mike understood—he felt the same way.

Goran's attention was caught momentarily by something in the waves, and Mike took advantage of that to slip off the bench and to the little open area in the middle of the semicircle. He dropped to one knee and waited for Goran to look his way.

Goran did—maybe because he noticed their companions' sudden silence. His mouth dropped open. "Mike?"

Mike pulled a small box from his jacket pocket. "I know we're already married in Nenahde, Gor. But I'd like to make it official here too. I'd like a California wedding, with rings and cake and tuxes and the whole nine yards." He flipped the box open to reveal the ring he'd bought. It was a plain wide band of black tungsten and silver. "Um, but before I ask you formally, um...." He cleared his throat, closed his eyes, and opened his mouth.

And in his terribly off-key voice—and in front of an audience of five, plus any eavesdropping gods—Mike sang Etta James. "At last...." It was awful. His low notes bottomed out, the high notes squawked, and the notes in between wobbled all over the place. And by the end of the song he was crying again, dammit. So was Mom and—to Mike's later amusement—Cleve.

But Goran only smiled. And when the song was mercifully over, Mike said, "Will you marry me, Goran? Again?" and Goran threw himself onto his knees so they could embrace. Mike almost lost the ring in the fierceness of it, but Marie charged over to grab the box and save the day.

"Of course I'll marry you, Mike," Goran said. "How could I not marry a man who'd sing like that for me?"

"It was a sacrifice. I wanted you to know how much I mean it."

Mike was an ordinary guy with an extraordinary lover. He believed that together they'd have a long, happy life, the strands of their fates woven indelibly together. He had learned one thing for certain: there was no use continuing to disbelieve in fantasy when you were living one every day.

And, oh yeah. True love? It turned out that was real too.